CHELSEY'S GIFT

R. D. KORVEMAKER

Another Day in Benton, Book One

CHELSEY'S GIFT

This is a work of fiction. Names, characters, places and incidents either are the product of the author's imagination or are used fictitiously, and any resemblance to actual persons, living or dead, businesses, companies, events, or locales is entirely coincidental.

ISBN: 978-1-4866-0884-3

Word Alive Press
131 Cordite Road, Winnipeg, MB R3W 1S1
www.wordalivepress.ca

Cataloguing in Publication may be obtained through Library and Archives Canada

To Sarah,

Thank you for reading and loving this story over and over again. Thank you for believing I could do it and pushing me on. This book would not be here without you.

"Trust in the Lord and do good; dwell in the land and befriend faithfulness...Commit your way to the Lord; trust in him, and he will act."

—Psalm 37:3, 5

ACKNOWLEDGEMENTS

I would like to thank the following for reading this book and sharing their honest thoughts and encouragement: Erin Koning (for your initial editing job), Steve De Boer, Jeff Schmitt, and Hannah Korvemaker. Without your support and ideas, this book would not be. Thank you.

CHAPTER ONE

It was one of those days—the kind that is both the beginning of one thing and the ending of something else. The park between Baldwin Street and Harris Street sat quietly after the community Labour Day picnic. Summer seemed to be sighing, thankful for the break as the people fled to their houses with too much food inside their bodies and too much sweat outside. The houses now contained sleeping fathers and mothers, and children calmly sitting before television screens, all taking a break before the fireworks started later that evening. The yellow house, however, spat out a lone runner into the quiet surroundings, and then licked its lips as the screen door slammed behind her.

Blue gym shorts, a gray T-shirt, and a blond ponytail raced down Baldwin Street. The runner was five-foot-four and her form was not exceptionally large or small but large-boned. She pushed a wisp of hair away from her eyes and kept up her steady pace.

She passed the convenience store where the sign for "Fireworks" still hung in the window. She turned down Apple Lane and passed her aunt and uncle's house. The lace curtains waved at her through the open window and the rocking chair on the front deck nodded as she passed. The town hall's bells rang out the time, *dong, dong, dong, dong, dong*. The runner smiled and sped on. Mom would expect her home for dinner soon. She rounded another corner to make it back to her block and passed the park again. A teen had interrupted the scene, throwing a Frisbee for his little dog. The runner glanced his way, breathing heavily in the sticky, August air. *Just a few more feet*. Then she was mounting the front steps of the yellow house again, bursting in the door, and pulling off her sweaty shoes.

"Kailey, you look gross."

She looked up and smiled at what could have been her reflection. "Thanks Chelsey, you're the best twin a girl could ask for."

"Oh good, because Dad says God doesn't take refunds."

Kailey gave her sister a slimy side hug and then darted up the stairs to the shower while Chelsey made a commotion from where she sat at the living room table. Devin, their little brother, told Chelsey to climb up the stairs herself if she wanted revenge. But Chelsey refused. She wouldn't, couldn't, climb up all sixteen of those steps to get to her sister, because she was afraid. No one knew why Chelsey had been afraid to climb steps her entire fifteen years, but then again, Chelsey was no ordinary child.

Kailey braided her damp hair and walked into the kitchen. She sniffed, then inhaled more deeply. Stir fry. She looped the hair elastic around the end of her braid and walked up behind Mom, who was standing before the stove with a massive wooden spoon in one hand and a bottle of soy sauce in the other. Cindy Martin was of average height with straight, long blond hair. The apron tied around her waist cut a line between faded denim shorts and a loose T-shirt that said something about being the world's best gardener on the back.

Kailey snuck up behind her and said loudly, "That smells good."

To her disappointment, Mom didn't so much as flinch. "Well, that's good because it's what you will be eating shortly. Please set the table," she said without turning her soft blue eyes from the wok.

"You're no fun."

Mom turned and raised her eyebrow. "No, I just have eyes in the back of my head."

Kailey gave Mom a peck on the check. "Five plates?"

Mom stirred her masterpiece of rice, chicken, and vegetables. "I think so."

Blue, brown, and cream-coloured plates descended from the cupboard beside the sink. Kailey pulled the checkered tablecloth straight and then laid out the mismatched set. Glasses, forks, a pitcher of lemon water, and a hot plate slid into their places. Kailey took the bouquet of wildflowers from the centre of the table and left them on the counter beside the screen door. She stopped and looked past the deck into the backyard. Devin had abandoned the model he'd been working on all afternoon to help Dad move the picnic table. They both sidestepped at the same time and Kailey couldn't help think how much they looked alike with their dark hair, deep blue eyes, and stocky build. Devin was just missing the mustache. Dad looked up as they set the table down, and waved. She stuck out her tongue.

Mom walked past her and hit her on the head with an oven mitt. "Go find your sister, you goof."

Kailey rubbed the top of her head. "Okay, okay, stop the abuse, I'm going." She walked away, sneaking a piece of chicken from the fry pan on her way.

"Hey!" Mom threw an oven mitt that hit the doorframe beside Kailey's head. She let out a little scream and darted into the living room.

The first floor of the Martins' home lent itself to be like a circle. The front door opened to face a wide flight of stairs up to the second floor with a hallway to the right of the stairs and a large, open living room to the left. Both the hallway and living room led directly to the kitchen at the back of the house. The hallway on the right had two doors. The first led to Dad's office at the front of the house, the second to Chelsey and Kailey's bedroom. The kitchen at the back served double duty as the dining room. A large bathroom with a full bath and laundry came off the far side of the kitchen. The living room, to the right of the entrance, supported a bay window and seat at the front of the house, letting in a considerable amount of light. The living room boasted dark, solid wood furniture, an upright piano, two bookshelves, and a fireplace. A small cards table sat against one wall, cornered in by the couch, lazy boy, rocking chair, coffee table, and two end tables. A brightly coloured lamp of oranges and purples sat on top of the piano. It had been a gift from Dad to Mom for one of their anniversaries and it matched absolutely nothing, but Mom declared that she "loved it" so there it stayed. The large clock on the wall beside the door to the kitchen read 3:38 even though it was almost 6:00. Dad had declared that he hated the "tick tock" sound it made and had promptly taken the batteries out the day he moved in. Kailey smiled. That had been a long time ago.

She found her sister bent over the card table by the front window. A canvas sat quietly while its master worked on clothing it with brilliant colours. Crazy Daisy, Chelsey's affectionate cat, sat watching her mistress with a bored expression on her orange and brown face.

"Mom says it's time to eat."

Chelsey didn't look up. "Did she make fish?"

"No."

"It smells like fish."

"It's not, it's rice."

"I don't like fish."

"Chelsey, only weird people like fish."

"I'm weird."

"Not when it comes to not liking fish. I think you're pretty normal about that."

Chelsey looked up and squinted. The twins were identical in their stature, strawberry blond curls, round faces, and the dimple that played hide and seek in their right cheek. Physically people had a hard time telling them apart. *Until they get to know us,* Kailey thought.

"But I am weird, aren't I, Kailey?" Her sister's eyes held questions and a demand for the answers.

"Chelsey, everyone is weird. Don't let people be mean to you because they don't like the way you are. *I* like the way you are. Come on, let's eat. What are you painting?"

Chelsey stood and wrinkled her nose at the picture. "A fish."

She walked away to the kitchen and left Kailey staring at her work. *No, not everyone is nice, especially to people like Chelsey. I wish they could look past her disability and see the person inside.* She sighed. *School starts tomorrow. Grade ten and the battle begins again.*

"Kailey! We are eating without YOU!"

She turned on her heel and ran into the kitchen. Each day had enough trouble of its own. Why borrow trouble from tomorrow? It would come soon enough.

CHAPTER TWO

The town of Benton, Ontario, sits twenty kilometers south of Lake Superior and forty kilometers east of the American border, with a three-hour drive east to Toronto thanks to the 402 and 401 highways. The land itself is flat—flat like set Jell-O, flat like a calm lake, flat like play dough a four-year-old has run over seventeen times with his Tonka truck. Woodland dots the farms, breaking up the flatness and providing a habitat for raccoons, deer, coyotes, rabbits, skunks, foxes, mice, squirrels, and the occasional groundhog. Blue jays, sparrows, crows, mourning doves, oriels, robins, herons, and cardinals live in the forests and ponds. Lake Superior aids the geese and swans and provides the most spectacular sunsets—reds, yellows, and purples spreading over the flat, flat land.

The summers are hot and humid and the winters offer snow, ice, bright sunshine, snow, pond hockey, cross-country skiing, and more snow. Benton boasts a population of five thousand people—at least that's what the welcome sign says on Highway 92. The majority of these people are farmers and tradesmen with teachers, preachers, retired farmers and tradesmen, hairdressers, bankers, and even a couple artists and musicians mixed in. From the sky the town itself looks like a grid. Highway 92 turns into Broadway Street and travels right down the middle of town with various avenues crossing it. The grocery and hardware stores, bank, library, and post office are on the east side of Broadway and the tractor dealership, Doug's Mechanic, the credit union, drug store, and Miss Betty's hair salon are on the west. The grade school and high school are on the north end of town and the second tractor dealership is in the south. The rest of the businesses—a radio station, Frank's Mechanic, two convenient stores, and several in-home hairdressing salons—are mixed in between the houses.

Despite the flatness all around Benton, two streets own hills: Baldwin Street and Apple Lane, running parallel. The bottom of the hill sits on Erie Street and the top levels out on Brock Street.

In such a flat place, most would have been happy to live on Baldwin Street. A hill would surely be a treat. That was the thinking behind a newly married couple's decision to purchase a home at the bottom of the hill. They smiled with love as they signed their names on the deed and moved in the furniture. She would rub her expanding middle and he would massage her sore feet and tell her of all the fun their twins would have. They waited and prayed and traveled up and down their hill; little did they know the trouble it would cause their babies.

"Chelsey, come on! The bus is going to leave before we get up the hill!"

"Bye Mom! Love you! Make us cookies, please!"

Kailey pulled her sister out the front door. "Seriously."

Chelsey gripped the railing with one hand and Kailey with the other. They slowly descended the three front steps. Chelsey was huffing and puffing by the time they landed on the pavement.

"You do know that we'll be doing this every day until the end of June, right?" Kailey adjusted her backpack and the knapsack on her shoulder and then took her sister's hand again.

"I know, but it's hard. I don't like it." Chelsey looked at her sister with big, sad blue eyes.

"I can't do anything about it, Chels." Kailey smiled at her gently. Chelsey nodded. She wasn't good with hills. Before the twins were born, there had been complications with Chelsey. Her muscles hadn't developed like they should have and her mind was slow compared to most children. As she grew, her muscles still didn't develop properly, making climbing difficult. Her parents had taken her to doctors and physiotherapists. At fifteen, she still visited the chiropractor and therapist monthly. Even though she was able to do more physically than the doctors had thought upon her birth, her mind stayed locked up in a child's world. She processed new concepts slowly, making math and science difficult. Her speech, however, was not greatly affected. Her communication was good, even though she wasn't always aware of what she was communicating.

"Do you think it will snow, Kailey?" Chelsey asked.

"It's September. It better not snow." Kailey bounced their bags, carrying her own and Chelsey's.

"Oh." She frowned and then smiled. "I like snow because I like to make snowmen! But I like jumping in leaves, too. Maybe we could make a leaf-man. Do you want to make a leaf-man?"

"Well, it will take a few weeks before the leaves start falling, too, and then when they do how will you get them to stick together?"

Chelsey scratched her head. "How does the tree do it?"

"Oh the trees leaves stick to sticks."

"Well, then we will get sticks."

"But why do you think the leaves fall in the first place? It's because the sticks aren't sticky anymore." Kailey's eyes sparkled as she looked at her sister.

"Oh..."

Behind them a garage door squeaked open.

"Here comes Logan, right on time," Kailey muttered.

A bike groaned in protest as someone hopped onto it and began a *tick-tick* sound as someone pedaled up behind them.

"He is not right on time. He is late," Chelsey corrected. The sun was already hot on their faces. It hungrily lay upon the grassy lawns to consume the dew that had settled there so peacefully the evening before. The dew had just started making its way to the earth when the Martin family had risen from watching the fireworks at the park. Chelsey wondered what happened to the fireworks that fell from the sky. Did they just disappear in the air or did they fall to the earth? Were they poisonous? Were they small enough for bugs and frogs to eat them so they didn't bother people? What would happen if a frog ate a piece of firework? They were almost to the top of the hill. Chelsey put her hand on her chest and took a deep breath. She turned to Kailey to ask but didn't get a chance.

"He's on time for Logan." Kailey's eyes clouded.

Logan Stewart lived next door with his parents. His mom worked as a property inspector and his father had a law partnership. Logan himself had been in the same grade as the twins since they moved from Toronto in grade seven. When his family had first moved next door, Mom and Dad had made a great effort to invite them over and try to get to know them. Eventually they stopped when it seemed to be ill received. They almost never saw his father, even at the beginning, because he seemed to be gone on business almost continually. His mother was a shy kind of lady with nervous mannerisms and hollow blue eyes. Logan never smiled. Nor did he ever have anything pleasant to say, not that he talked much. His dark hair, dark eyes, and dark expression made him a formidable individual.

They made it to the top of the hill as the bus pulled up. Logan had just finished locking his bike to a nearby fence. The twins waited as Logan pulled up his perpetually low, baggy jeans and climbed in, then Kailey lifted their bags into the front seat and helped Chelsey in. Mrs. Brown, the same bus driver they'd had in grade nine, welcomed them back to her bus with a nod and tiny smile. They took their seats and the yellow beast jerked forward. Kailey sighed. The bus smelled clean. No gum under the seats, no dirty socks, no apple cores or banana peels. First day of school, last day of clean bus, the journey of grade ten had begun.

Kailey looked out the window while Chelsey spread her time between chatting with Mrs. Brown and watching the other kids get on. Both girls stopped their activities when Amanda McGee entered and took the seat behind them.

"Hey ladies!" she said. "Chelsey, you look phenomenal! That green tee and light jean skirt are great! Who do you shop with? Maybe you could pass on some fashion tips to your sister here." Amanda jabbed a finger toward Kailey while maintaining eye contact with Chelsey. Amanda had been Kailey's best friend for as long as she could remember. When they were little, Amanda had always added a new level of noise and excitement to the Martin home. A picture Mom still kept of the fridge displayed the two of them at seven years old in their bathing suits. Kailey's hair stuck out from two curly red piggy tails on either side of her head and Amanda's brown wisps flew around her face. Kailey held a chocolate Popsicle and Amanda held up an empty stick while her face beamed, covered in chocolate Popsicle. Now that they were fifteen, Amanda still added noise and excitement to their home. Her hair had toned down but she still smiled a great deal and her chocolate Popsicles tended to at least make an appearance on her face.

Chelsey giggled. "I shop with her!"

"Well, perhaps you should give her some more help." Amanda winked at Kailey.

"I will do my best," Chelsey said and went back to her people watching.

Amanda leaned over and patted Kailey on the shoulder. "You are one hot grade tenner, too, girlfriend. Love the rolled-up-jeans look. It's good on you. Shows off your fantastic ankles."

Kailey laughed. "Well thank you, you know just what to say."

"Hey, what else are friends for?"

The bus swung around a corner and entered the school grounds. The front driveway was a paved circle with a section of lawn in the middle. This way the busses didn't need to back up after letting the students out. The parking lot was situated on the west side of the school building. Behind the school lay the sports field and picnic tables. The bus jerked to a stop.

"Kailey, I'll see you at lunch. Chelsey, you're in my home Ec class. I've just got to run something to the office. See you guys in a bit!" Amanda pulled her bag onto her shoulder and hurried off the bus.

Chelsey took Benton High's program for handicap children when it came to the core courses, like math and science, but took the regular art classes. Kailey waited for the other kids to get off before helping her twin down the bus steps.

Kailey again shouldered their bags and looked up at the school. It was a three-story, red brick building with tall windows and high front steps. Logan and his gang of friends had already taken their usual place beside the bike racks and mocked whomever they pleased as the other students made their way into the school. Kailey took a deep breath and walked forward.

"Hey! The retards are back!" Bret Thomas called from beside Logan. "Look guys, the look-a-like retards are back for another year!"

One of his friends, Jeff Buffet, slapped him on the back and laughed.

"I wonder how it feels to look retarded all the time," Lori White, Logan's girlfriend, said. "Hey! Have you ever tried talking to a brick wall? It would be like looking at a better version of you with better conversation skills."

Kailey pulled Chelsey around to the back of the school where they could enter using the ramp instead of the stairs. She wished her twin hadn't heard all that. It wasn't like she hadn't heard insults before; it was just a crummy way to start school. But Chelsey never complained when people were mean. She simply ducked her head and walked on. It was almost as if she chose not hear the words, to ignore the people who laughed at her because of her differences. Instead of getting angry, she'd continue with her life, painting her pictures and singing her songs.

The inside of the school was painted with tone colours. Not the nice kind of tone colours with proper accents and rustic decorations that you would see in a creative woman's home. These tone colours looked like they were just whatever was on sale when the head of the maintenance committee went to Home Hardware. Some walls were an off-white, some were a soft brown, one entire classroom was a beige-green. As if to catch a visitor completely by surprise, the gym was a faded pink. Perhaps that was the committee's original strategy to win on home turf. Now, however, since most rival teams had already competed in the gym it was no longer an advantage for the Benton Bears but fuel for mockery against them. When students transferred to other schools, they'd inevitably be asked, "Is that the school with the cotton candy gym?"

Steel lockers lined the hallways like guards on duty. Long fluorescent lights screwed to the ceiling flooded the hallways with bright, unnatural light. Heavy wood doors opened to classrooms. The classrooms also had fluorescent lights but they contained mostly natural light thanks to large windows. The classrooms were not only brighter than the hallways, they also smelled different. The hallways permeated the smell of lemons, pine, and bleach thanks to the different cleaning supplies Mr. Kay, the janitor, used. The classrooms, however, all smelled different. The English, History, and Literature rooms smelled like books, the science lab smelled like dirt and formaldehyde and the lemon tree that stood by the window like a class pet, and the art room gave off the continual sent of paint and permanent markers.

Kailey and Chelsey rounded the corner and located their lockers. Kailey pulled everything out of her bag that she wouldn't need for the first period and shoved it into her locker, then proceeded to do the same with Chelsey's stuff. "So you're in Home Ec first period and I'm going to English. Amanda's in your class."

Chelsey rolled her eyes and sighed heavily. "You don't have to worry about me. I did this *every day* last year."

"I know, but I still worry. Amanda will walk you to the Learning Centre after Home Ec. Her class is right across the hall, so you can go to lunch with her. I'll meet you at lunch."

Chelsey frowned, picked up her bag, and marched down the hallway toward her first class. Kailey ran to catch up and walked with her to her first class. She settled her disgruntled sister and fled to get to her own class on time. English 10 with Mr. Marskdale. She'd been in his class last year, too. He seemed like a nice teacher, other than the fact that he enjoyed English. *Wonder if he'll have a bowtie today or a regular tie.* She ran down the hallway and up a flight of stairs. *I hope Mazie saved me a seat beside her. Wonder what she did this summer.* She turned the corner and banged into someone. She stumbled back and looked up into the blue eyes of the blond boy standing five inches taller than her.

"Oh, sorry," she managed to say as she caught her breath.

"Hey, no worries," he said.

"Excuse me." She smiled, stepped around him, and continued down the hall at a power-walk instead of a run. Students scurried around, finding their rooms. Kailey walked into 212 and took the desk beside Mazie. Summer hadn't changed her English class buddy a bit. Her hair was still a mix of bright pink and dark purple tied back with two hair elastics on the top of her head. Five clips of differing sizes and colours and a bright green bandana held all her stray wisps away from her face. Her left ear faced Kailey, displaying four piercings.

"How was your summer?" Kailey asked.

"Hot. What else does summer do?" Mazie smacked her gum and dusted the crumbs from what must have been breakfast off her tie-dye shirt.

"Mazie, did you make your shirt?"

"No, Gram won't let me use the stove and I think you gotta heat up the dye. I got it from the thrift store with Gramps when he was looking for a couch or something. He was keener on the tie-dye shirt than the tattoo I wanted to get. Did you know in this part of Ontario you have to be *sixteen* before you can get a tattoo—and that's with parental consent?"

"You were going to get a tattoo at the thrift store?"

"And my grandparents are never gonna sign for me to have a tattoo, so I'm going to have to wait till I'm *eighteen*. That's pretty much old. Wait, what?" Mazie's eyebrows knit together. "You can't get a tattoo at the thrift store. Talk about sketchy." She blew another bubble.

"Well, you can get weight loss pills at the dollar store."

"Really?"

Kailey nodded.

"Well that's sketchy too."

"Good morning, class!" Mr. Marksdale walked in with a briefcase and a smile entirely too large for 9:00 am. *Bowtie—brown and blue polka-dotted bowtie.* Kailey guessed him to be in his late fifties. His curly hair was losing the battle with his forehead and his round glasses sat on the bridge of his nose. He had three great loves that his classes generally didn't share: mornings, English, and his students. He stood by his desk, opened his briefcase, and began sorting papers. Once he found what he was searching for, he looked up and smiled again. "Welcome to English 10. We're going to start with a general review from English 9. I will hand out these sheets and give you twenty minutes to go through the questions. Don't sweat if you don't know—hello, Mr. Stewart."

All heads turned to the doorway, where Logan was standing with his bag over his shoulder.

"Please come in and take your seat behind Miss Martin. Please don't be late again."

The class waited while Logan took his seat behind Kailey. She felt a shadow loom over her as he sat down. She shivered. Mr. Marksdale passed out the papers and she searched for a pen. "Mazie? Do you have a pen I could borrow?"

Mazie reached into her hair and pulled one out. Without taking her eyes off her paper, she handed it to Kailey. Mr. Marksdale told them to begin and all the heads bent over their work. Kailey shivered again, pulled her blue sweater closer, and focused on diagramming sentences.

CHAPTER THREE

Chelsey glared at the computer screen. Computers were D.U.M.B. as far as she was concerned. Her dad didn't know much about computers, and he was a fine fellow, so why should she need to know anything about them? She figured she could make out fine without this kind of harassment, just like Daddy. She growled as a sign popped up on her screen. "You are the dumbest thing I have *ever* had to use!" she told the screen. "I hope I never have to see you again as a long as I live!"

"Having trouble, Chelsey?" Mr. Smith, one of the Special Ed supply teachers came to stand behind her chair. He was a tall, lanky man with blond hair that was thinning *everywhere*. Chelsey figured he was just about as old as her dad and therefore classified him in the almost-ancient category.

"This thing," she said, motioning to the screen dramatically, "just popped up on me and I don't know what to do with it." She looked up at him with pleading blue eyes. "Will you fix it?"

The bell rang.

Mr. Smith smiled. "Sure. You go have lunch."

"Thanks! See you later!" Chelsey gave him her biggest smile, showing all her teeth, and hurried out of the room to meet Amanda. She'd had enough of technology for one day.

She waited in the hallway while students filed out of the classroom across the hall. "Kailey said to wait for Amanda," she whispered to herself. "I will wait." She tapped her foot and looked up, out the window, up, then back at the wall. The ceiling was still white and the walls were still gray. Her foot tapped faster. All of Amanda's classmates had filed out. What was taking her so long?

"And people say I move slowly," Chelsey muttered under her breath.

A movement outside the window caught her eye. She watched a sparrow fly before the glass with a large leaf in its mouth. It struggled, dodging back and forth, and then suddenly took off for the evergreens on the south side of the building. Chelsey continued to watch till it was out of sight. She sighed heavily and then jumped.

"What are you looking at?" Amanda asked, standing beside her.

"A bird."

"Oh. Ready for lunch?" she asked, pushing her hair out of her face.

Chelsey nodded and started down the hall. "I'm hungry. Do you know what this school needs?"

"Better internet?"

"Murals," Chelsey said. "The colours are all boring."

Amanda looked around her; white, gray, brown. "I guess. You know what I need? The bathroom."

Chelsey sighed again and rolled her eyes. "I am really, *really* hungry. Could you please go as quickly as possible?"

"You should go, too. You know you're going to need to in about fifteen minutes." Amanda pushed open the heavy wooden door. A stickperson proudly sporting a skirt was screwed on the outside.

"No I won't," Chelsey said and went to lean against the wall by the drinking fountain. At this rate they were never going to get any lunch. The kitchen staff would have everything cleaned up. Then they would just walk back to class. She would have spent the entire dinner period waiting in the hall.

"Why the frown, brown cow?" Amanda asked, emerging from the bathroom.

"Can we please go eat? I am really hungry. We're not going to get any food."

"Yup, and it's the first day of school so there's bound to be something good."

They turned the corner and entered the cafeteria. Amanda took two trays and handed one to Chelsey. "If you really think we need murals, maybe you should tell the principle. Mr. Woodford is a pretty cool guy. I bet he would go for it."

"Pizza."

"Pizza murals?"

"Look." Chelsey pointed ahead to where one of the kitchen staff was putting two slices of pizza on a student's plate.

"Oh, yum!" Amanda bounced once to let out her excitement.

"Wait, did you just say Principle Woodford is a cool guy?" Chelsey wrinkled her nose.

"Never mind. Chels, do you see that guy over there?"

Chelsey turned around. "Where?"

"The one by the window reading a book. Blond hair, blue T-shirt, jeans, looking bored."

Chelsey shook her head.

"The cute one."

Chelsey stuck her tongue out at her friend.

Amanda glared at her. "Come on, do you see who I mean? That guy who looks new."

"Oh, the guy we don't know?" Chelsey asked brightly.

"Yes."

"Yeah, should we eat with him?"

"With who?" Kailey came up behind them with a tray in her hand.

"That cute guy over there sitting by the window."

Kailey's eyes grew when she saw who Amanda was referring to. "We can't eat with that guy," she whispered.

"Why not? He probably doesn't have any friends," Amanda said.

"Boys should be friends with him." Kailey took a slice of cheese pizza off the tray. "And I almost plowed him over in the hallway this morning."

"Seriously?" Amanda stared at her. "Do tell!"

Chelsey ignored them and got her pizza. She wasn't fond of boys in general. They tended to smell weird. She scanned the room and made a beeline for Maria Berry, who was sitting alone. She took a seat at the corner of the table and Maria smiled and slid over to sit next to her. Maria had been their friend since grade four when she had moved to Benton from Hamilton. Her grandmother had lived in Benton at the time, and the family had decided to move so they could live with her. Grandma Berry had been a merry sort of person with white hair and wrinkles and she smelled like moth balls. Due to her old age, she hadn't be able to live alone anymore. She had passed away just after they graduated from grade eight, Chelsey thought.

One of the best things about Maria was the fact that she had three older brothers: Terrence, Colin, and Rob. Other than her own little brother, these were the only boys Chelsey actually liked. For one thing they usually smelled clean and for another they liked to play. They played anything—Memory and Go Fish with Chelsey, soccer and volleyball with Maria and Kailey. They climbed trees and played hide-and-seek and they made the biggest snowmen Chelsey had ever seen. Maria also had two older sisters, but they had grown up and gotten married and moved out west so Chelsey didn't see them often.

"Hi Maria, how are you?" Chelsey asked.

"Good. How were your classes this morning? What did you have?" Maria asked in her calm, singsong voice.

"I had Home Ec and then Computers. What about you?"

"World History and then Geometry," Maria said. Her blond hair was pulled back in a French braid down her back.

Amanda and Kailey joined them. Amanda took a seat next to Chelsey, and Kailey slid in next to Maria.

"So, is Rob going to help us practice for volleyball after school?" Kailey asked.

"Rob left for university yesterday," Maria replied.

"Wow, that's the last of your brothers to move out, isn't it?" Amanda pulled the pepperoni off her pizza. "Who wants this?"

"I will!" Kailey held out her hand.

"Yeah, he's the last one. They're all gone now. The house is quiet. Mom said she's going to start playing the home videos from when we were younger so there's noise again."

"That would be entertaining," Amanda offered around a mouthful of pizza. "Ladies, this is going to be our last good meal of the year. After this it's back to bologna sandwiches and cucumber slices."

"I like bologna," Chelsey said.

"Are you going to try out for volleyball again this year?" Kailey asked Maria.

"I want to. I think we can get in now that we're in grade ten."

With that they were off. Amanda rolled her eyes and smiled at Chelsey. They both knew there was no hope of reclaiming the conversation. Amanda even interjected that she might try out for cheerleading in the hopes of changing the topic, but neither girl seemed to notice. Chelsey ate her pizza and then worked on her pudding, listening to Maria and Kailey discuss who else might be on their team and if they'd get Coach Davis or Coach Willis, hoping they'd get the former.

By the time they'd all finished their food, Chelsey was also finished with conversation. "I need to use the washroom," she declared.

This statement caused the girls to quiet.

"I told you to go when I went because you'd need to in like fifteen minutes," Amanda said.

"It's been like forty-five minutes, Amanda," Kailey said, checking her watch. "Come on Chelsey, I have to go too. See you girlies later."

After their pit stop, the twins walked back to the Special Ed room and then Kailey went to biology. Chelsey endured math and then had a spare. Kailey, Maria, and Amanda all had classes while Chelsey was in spare, so she took out her pencil crayons and did some sketching. After spare, she made her way down the hallway to art class. Her favourite class. She sat near the front. Other students filtered in, the last being Logan Stewart. Through the whole class, Logan didn't say anything and Chelsey was grateful. He never said anything nice to her, so it was better if he didn't speak at all. After class, she waited for Kailey and then they walked to the bus together. She was grateful as Kailey helped her up to her seat. Why buses had so many steps was beyond her understanding. She sat quietly on the way home. Day one was over. Only 194 left to go.

Those 194 days that made up the school year slowly dwindled away. Kailey ran after each school day. Chelsey painted. And both twins groaned when they contemplated the next day's climb up the hill.

"Seven plates tonight."

Kailey turned from her place at the cupboard and raised her left eyebrow.

Mom saw the question on her face. "Aunt Louise and Uncle Bruno are coming for supper."

"Yes!" Kailey said in delight. "Mom, you're the best mother there ever was. I love you!" She gave her mother a peck on the cheek and then took down two extra plates and set them on the table.

Uncle Bruno and Aunt Louise lived on Apple Lane, a couple blocks away from the Martins. They had met online four years ago and had gotten married last summer. It would have been a challenge to find a couple who were more different. Uncle Bruno was a large, burly kind of man with a deep laugh and mischievous glow about him. He shared his opinions freely, which was probably partly why he worked as a radio host. Aunt Louise was a quiet, petite woman. She taught swimming lessons out of their home, which had an indoor pool.

Kailey set the honey-coloured oak table with plates, glasses, forks, spoons, knives, a pitcher of water, napkins, and potholders. She retrieved the salt and pepper shakers from their place in the corner cupboard and left them close to Dad's place at the head of the table. The kitchen was painted in light yellow and the oak cupboards matched the table. It always smelled good in this room. Except when Mom felt the urge to fix fish. Whenever she did that she would also light a candle to help remove the smell; but then it just smelled like fishy candle.

Kailey had just finished setting the table when she heard a knock on the door and then a squeak as it opened. "Is anybody home?" a deep voice bellowed. "Because even if you're not, something sure smells good and I will be happy to eat it all."

Kailey smiled at Mom and walked into the living room. Her uncle stood in the entranceway—in fact he *filled* it with his six-foot-four frame. A head full of red hair with a full beard to match gave away his Scottish heritage. A small finger came from behind him and poked his shoulder and then a sweet, tranquil voice said, "Dear, would you please move? I would like to see the lovely people we came to visit."

"Well," said Uncle Bruno, "they're nothing special to look at."

Kailey frowned at his wink and put her hands on her hips.

"All the same, this pie does need to go in the fridge."

"Oh!" Uncle Bruno stepped into the hallway and let his elfin, brown-haired wife get by. Aunt Louise was the opposite of Uncle Bruno in every way, from her small stature to her calm, quiet presence. She said her national background was that of a mutt—a good mix of everything, but most of all she declared herself to be Canadian.

"Hello Kailey, how are you?" Aunt Louise had a way of asking questions and looking at people like she really, truly cared about how they would answer.

"Just swell. I'm so glad you can come for dinner. I mean, I was a bit disappointed to see Uncle Bruno, but I guess it's not really wise to leave him home alone. I suppose we could maybe find a soup bone or something for him to chew on."

"You're right, dear, he doesn't do so well in that house by himself. I'll see if your mother has something to keep him occupied while we have dinner." Aunt Louise patted her on the arm with a warm look in her eyes as she passed Kailey on her way to the kitchen.

Uncle Bruno faked a hurt expression. "Well, did you happen to know that soup bones are my favourite?"

"Really?" Kailey's eyes danced.

"No, I lied. I do like pretty much everything, though." The rocking chair gasped and croaked as Bruno took his seat. He clasped his hands behind his head and closed his eyes. "Come now, lassie. Play me a song on your instrument and I shall forgive you and then we can eat whatever delicious food your mother has prepared."

Kailey took a seat at the piano and began to play her own version of *Twinkle, Twinkle Little Star*. Her right hand started two octaves above middle C and her touch was light.

"Ah, lass, that's lovely," Uncle Bruno murmured.

Out of the corner of her eye, Kailey saw Devin descending from his room on the second story. Her eyes abandoned the instrument altogether and turned to watch her little brother. His dark hair and eyes and stocky build compared to his father's, but his smile was a gift from Mom. He slowly made his way across the hardwood floor in his wool socks, swinging his arms out slowly to keep his balance as he tiptoed. When his feet met the rug, he moved a bit more quickly with a brief stop and then a large step over where he knew the floor made a creaking noise.

And then he jumped.

Uncle Bruno, who had really been watching with one eye partially open, caught him and swung him up in the air, declaring that the whole family must be against him, wooing him with music and then attacking him while he slept. Uncle Bruno was, of course, much bigger than his nephew, but he let Devin wrestle with him until Devin sat on him with his arm twisted behind his back and his face in the rug. Kailey cheered for Devin from her place on the piano bench.

Chelsey came in from the kitchen and looked down at the spectacle. Devin grinned. "I captured the bear," he said.

"Devin, you are one brave man," she said sarcastically.

"Kids!"

Kailey looked toward the kitchen and then back at the boys on the floor. "Well, now I think Mom wants to feed the bear."

Uncle Bruno stood up and swung Devin under his arm. "Well then, let's go!"

Kailey and Chelsey followed. Uncle Bruno set Devin down in his chair and then took the chair beside him.

"Have you boys gotten out all your energy now? Do you think you can sit still while we eat?" Mom asked in a serious tone, but her eyes sparkled.

Devin and Uncle Bruno nodded, their spirits obviously subdued.

Dad sat at the head of the table and laughed. "Good," he said. "Let's pray." And with that they all sat and joined hands.

CHAPTER FOUR

Logan Stewart stood before the kitchen stove with a spatula in one hand. The pan before him sizzled and snapped. He carefully slid the spatula under the bottom piece of bread and flipped. A beautiful brown appeared, glowing from the butter he had spread on it. While he waited for the other side to finish, he went to the fridge and retrieved the ketchup bottle. Grilled cheese without ketchup just wasn't acceptable. His Irish Terrier, Nog, barked in the backyard. Logan found a plate and went back to the stove.

Mitch, Logan's older brother, walked to the screen door beside the fridge and yelled. "Shut it, you dumb dog!"

"Hey, don't yell at him." Logan flipped his sandwich onto his plate.

Mitch shuffled over to the coffeemaker and looked up with bloodshot eyes. "I'll yell at your dog if I want to."

"You don't even live here, why do you care?"

"Because that damn dog woke me up, that's why."

Logan leaned over the island counter. "Yell at my dog and I'll tell Mom you've been drinking again."

Mitch glared at him over his mug.

Logan took his plate and went to the basement to play computer games. Saturday. It was early, before 10:30, so he knew none of his friends would be out of bed yet. He ate his breakfast and played for the next three hours. Bret called and asked if he wanted to go to the convenient store and "get some food." Logan agreed to meet him and Jeff there in thirty minutes. Saturdays. He threw a bone to Nog on his way out the door, promising to come back to take him for a walk later, then he hopped on his bike and made his way down the street.

"What do you need?" Kailey asked, leaning against the kitchen counter. She reached over Mom and snatched an apple out of the fruit basket.

"Crème of tartar," Mom replied, handing her a pink ten-dollar bill and a blue five.

"What's that used for?" Chelsey asked from the kitchen table.

"Baking. Can you also pick up a dozen eggs?"

"Sure, but I don't think Mr. Smee has crème of tartar at the variety store."

"If he doesn't, go down to Aunt Louise and see if she has any."

"Okay." Kailey stood. "Come on, Chelsey, let's go."

"But what are you baking?" Chelsey asked, getting off her chair.

"Key lime pie," Mom answered.

"What's a key lime?"

"He's a cousin to lemon meringue. Now go with your sister," Mom said.

"Okay, Mom." Chelsey yawned. Her muscles hurt; they had tightened up in the night, which meant she hadn't slept well. She walked through the living room where Dad was reading the newspaper. He looked up at her and smiled. No smile came in reply.

"Bye Dad," she said glumly.

"Bye pumpkin, have fun. Protect your sister from the bad guys," Dad said gently and patted her hand as she walked by.

"Okay, I'll try."

Chelsey shuffled to the front entranceway where Kailey stood waiting. She slid into her sandals and then took Kailey's outreached hand. She slowly descended the front steps. *Why do we live in a house that has front steps? Why didn't Mom and Dad buy a house that I could just walk into and not have to climb steps at all?* She kept her hand in Kailey's as they walked down the street toward Mr. Smee's store. Chelsey kicked every stone between their house, number 79 Baldwin Street, and the variety store, number 23.

"Chelsey, are you okay?"

"I don't want to go to the store."

"I know."

"How do you know?"

"Because you're frowning like someone ran over Crazy Daisy."

"Why did I have to go with you?"

"Dad said you had to protect me from the bad guys," Kailey said.

Chelsey sniffed. "I don't know how to fight bad guys."

"Hmm, maybe you should tell Dad that and he can sign you up for karate lessons or something."

"I don't want to do that either," Chelsey moaned and let out a sob.

Kailey stopped. "Chelsey, *what is wrong?*"

"I don't know!" Chelsey howled, and with that tears poured out of her eyes.

Kailey gave her a hug and waited. Chelsey cried for a full minute. She stopped and wiped her eyes on the back of her hand. Kailey watched her in silence.

Chelsey sniffed again. "Okay, I'm ready now. I feel better. Thank you."

"You're welcome. Want to talk about why you're upset?"

"I slept bad last night. And my muscles hurt."

"Oh." Kailey took her hand again as they continued on their journey.

"Sorry, Kailey, it's not nice to cry on the street."

Kailey's eyes met her own. "It's okay. Sometimes a girl's just got to cry."

Chelsey nodded. They walked on in silence. Squirrels jumped and ran between the maples that lined the sidewalk. They waved to Mr. Cho who was outside weeding his flowerbeds with his ugly dog Francis, a hairless Chinese Crested, at his side. Mr. Cho said once that he came from Korea thirty years ago. Now he looked to be somewhere in his sixties. He was a quiet man who liked to keep to himself. When Francis saw the girls, she jumped up on her short legs and ran toward them with ferocious intentions. Her bark was silenced when the leash clipped to her collar ran out.

"Francis!" Mr. Cho scolded.

"Hi Mr. Cho!" Kailey called. He returned her wave and then pulled his dog to stand before him so he could talk to her about her behavior. The girls walked on.

"He's weird."

"That's not nice, Chelsey."

"Devin says his dog's like a big, naked rat with a lion's mane on steroids. Stupid Francis."

"When did Dev say that?"

"After Uncle Bruno did."

Kailey rolled her eyes and pushed open the door to Mr. Smee's store. The bell above the door greeted them as they entered. Mr. Smee, a short man with white hair and square glasses, stood behind the counter wearing an apron, counting money. Even the counter and the apron couldn't disguise his rounding middle. His wife had worked as a chef before they had children. That was some thirty-plus years ago. Apparently she hadn't lost her touch.

"Hello, girls. How can I help you?" his tenor voice asked gently.

"Mom sent us for crème of tartar and eggs," Kailey replied.

Chelsey poked Kailey. "Can I look at the fish while you find the stuff?"

Kailey nodded.

Chelsey turned on her heel and walked toward the large fish tanks near the front window. There was a tank with different Goldfish, one with tropical fish, and her favourite tank: the South American Cichlids. A myriad of colours danced around each other, in and out of the water plants and sunken pirate ship: angel fish, ballooned belly mollies, bleeding heart tetras, comet goldfish, ghost shrimp, and many others, all close in size. The crab kept to himself at the bottom of the tank. "Crabs are always cranky," Chelsey muttered.

The bell above the door jingled again. Chelsey looked up and then quickly turned back to her fish friends. Logan, Bret, and Jeff had just entered. She heard Mr. Smee ask if they needed any help. One of them replied that they were "just looking" and then they all laughed and turned down the candy aisle. Chelsey kept her head turned to the fish tank. Wrappers crinkled, the boys laughed, zippers slid up and down, and then the boys walked away. *What are they doing? They just walked out and I don't think they paid for their candy!* Chelsey jumped when a hand touched her arm.

"What's up, cute duck?" Kailey asked. "I found the stuff and paid Mr. Smee. Let's get it to Mom so she can make key lime pie, whatever that is."

"Okay." Chelsey took her sister's hand again and opened the front door since Kailey's other hand was full. "Bye Mr. Smee, see you later."

"Bye girls." He waved, and the laugh lines around his eyes exploded as he smiled.

September in Southwestern Ontario has a mind of its own. The temperature fluctuates between 15°C and 32°C with the usual temperature in the early to mid 20s. Rain and sunshine compete for performing space in the theatre of the sky with the sun often winning more time. The farmers roll out their combines and prepare for October when the soybeans and corn are harvested, and once that's finished they take out their plows and planters to sow winter wheat to be harvested the following July. The trees slowly turn from green to red, yellow, and orange with a few stubborn ones refusing to turn any other colour at all and so they simply fall to the ground never experiencing the glory of the change.

Logan, Bret, and Jeff road their bikes to the park to meet Lori, Ashley, and Todd at the park. The day was 22°C with a slight breeze. Logan pulled his cap farther down to keep the sun out of his eyes while they pedaled down the sidewalk. They dropped their bikes on the ground next to a picnic table and pushed two ten-year-old boys off the swings before sharing their booty with the others.

"The old man didn't see you?" Todd, a skinny boy with brown hair and a dimpled left cheek, asked.

"No way man, we're old hands at this kind of thing." Bret punched Logan's shoulder and shoved a handful of skittles in his mouth.

"What would happen if you did get caught?" Todd asked.

"They'd end up in jail or juvie," Ashley said with a syrupy voice. She leaned her blond head against Jeff's shoulder and looked up at him. He kissed her forehead. She reached her left hand behind his head and brought it down to kiss him.

"They never get caught," Lori said.

"Hey Jeff, could you chill for a minute and toss me those M&Ms?" Bret asked.

Jeff pulled away from Ashley and threw the bag to Bret. "Anyone got any spray paint at home?"

"Why?"

"Why do you think? We could go down to the train station and have some fun."

"Oh." Todd nodded slowly.

"Look guys, I got to go." Logan got off the swing, causing Lori, who was sitting on his lap, to get up too. She took his seat. Logan leaned over to kiss her soundly and then stood and walked toward his bike.

"Where you going?"

"Home. I got stuff to do." Logan got on his bike and pedaled away.

"See you! My brother's coming home so I can lift some smokes off him for Monday," Jeff called after him.

"You got it!" Logan waved. Nog was still waiting for his walk, and Logan wanted some milk. Besides, he wasn't good at graffiti. Art wasn't his thing and graffiti was definitely some kind of art.

CHAPTER FIVE

"Well, I'm ugly," Kailey muttered to the girl who stared at her in the mirror. "Why art thou so puffy, hair, and why dost thou have a Siamese twin, oh thou chin?"

"What?" Chelsey yelled as she entered their bedroom. Her hair was still wet from her shower.

"I was talking to myself," Kailey replied in a less than jovial manner.

"Quoting Shakespeare?" Chelsey wrinkled her nose.

"Yes. How did you know?"

"You always quote Shakespeare on Sunday mornings." Chelsey went to their closet. "I don't know why. You don't even read Shakespeare. What are you going to wear today?"

"This?" Kailey turned in her chair.

Chelsey's head poked out from their walk-in closet. "You're going to wear an organ skirt with a black and gray striped shirt?"

"What's wrong with that, Miss oh-so-good-at-fashion?"

"You look like Halloween and it's not even October," Chelsey yelled back at her from somewhere in the recesses of the closet.

"Why don't you wear your blue skirt instead?"

Kailey stood and dragged herself to the closet. Inside, Chelsey was busy pulling blouses and skirts off their hangers. She held up a polka-dotted gray top and a long green skirt. "Oh, hi Kailey. I thought you were still by the mirror. I'm going to wear this."

Kailey's eyebrows raised. "I don't think that matches."

"Well you're the one walking around like a giant jack-o-lantern."

"Chelsey! I am not! This looks fine."

"Go ask Mom," she said and pulled on the skirt.

Kailey, feeling as if the world and her only sister were totally out to prove the point of her ugliness, left the bedroom and walked to the kitchen. "Mom?"

Mom stood beside the sink stirring her coffee. "Yes dear?"

"Do I look like a walking jack-o-lantern?" She gestured to her clothing choice.

Mom looked her up and down. "No, dear."

"I told Chelsey!" Kailey turned to walk back to their room.

"But you do look like Chelsey picked out your clothes,"

"With her eyes closed," Dad added as he entered from the living room.

Kailey let out a growl and stalked back to her room. She didn't say a word to Chelsey but made haste to the walk-in. "I *do not* look like a jack-o-lantern. I just look ugly. Jack-o-lanterns are ugly." She scanned the closet and then picked up her dark green pencil skirt. She pulled off the orange and pulled on the green. When she emerged she caught Chelsey's smile in the mirror. Choosing to ignore it she sat down before the mirror again and pulled her hair up into a messy bun with hair coming out in random places. "Whatever," she muttered again.

"Kailey, will you braid my hair?" Chelsey asked.

"Okay, sit down." Kailey stood and Chelsey took her place. The room was silent for a moment. Kailey was still upset over her appearance and Chelsey's head was beginning to hurt from the way her sister pulled on her hair.

Finally Chelsey ventured to ask, "What did Mom say?"

"Her and Dad said I looked like *you* helped me dress with your eyes closed," Kailey said around the bobby-pins in her mouth.

Chelsey gigged, ever so slightly, but it was still a giggle.

"It's not funny, Chelsey."

"Sorry." Chelsey tried to remain serious, but when Kailey looked up her eyes were laughing in the mirror, laughing so hard that small tears had started forming in their corners.

"Chelsey..." Kailey warned.

"I'm sorry, Kailey." Chelsey let out another small giggle. "I know you're angry. I would be angry, too, if I looked like a jack-o-lantern and no one told me before going to church. Imagine how hard it would be for

Pastor Liam to preach with a giant jack-o-lantern sitting there!" Chelsey could hold in her delight no longer. She doubled over and laughed. Kailey let go of her hair and waited for Chelsey to stop, but Chelsey couldn't stop. She laughed until she started to hiccup.

Kailey shook her head and walked away. *This is the stupidest day ever! Chelsey doesn't even know anything about fashion and here she is laughing at me because I look ridiculous. Even Mom and Dad think I look ridiculous! Now I look like a bloated balloon. What a stupid day. I hate clothes. Kailey, this is silly. Grow up. They were being honest with you and just because you're in a bad mood today doesn't mean everyone else has to be, too. If three people thought it was funny it must be slightly humorous. And Chelsey has a point, Pastor Liam would be distracted by that much orange and black.* With a smile, although a very small smile, playing on her lips, she turned back to her sister.

"You look better now," Chelsey assured her once her laughter had stopped and her hiccups had decreased. "Will you finish my hair?"

"Only if you promise to *always* tell me when I look like a jack-o-lantern before church," Kailey said, walking back to her unfinished project.

"Deal!"

Kailey quietly took her seat at the end of the pew. Dad would sit between her and Mom when he came with the other elders, the deacons, and Pastor Liam. On the other side of Mom sat Chelsey and then Devin. The church sanctuary sat up to five hundred people, but generally held the three hundred and fifty members of the congregation every Sunday, plus a handful of visitors. One aisle ran between the two long rows of benches and another aisle separated each section of benches from the outside wall. The walls were painted a light brown, matching the gray spotted carpet, and windows let in the natural light on both sides. The pulpit was made of quarter-sawn oak finished in a dark honey colour. To the right stood the baptismal font and the baby grand piano and to the left stood the Lord's Supper table and the organ. The baptismal font and Lord's Supper table were stained to match the pulpit. The ceiling arched high overhead. There were murmurs that a balcony could be put in at some point.

Mrs. Berry sat at the organ playing the prelude. The family with four little red-headed girls took their seats on the other side of the church.

Two of the widows were conversing loudly at the rear of the sanctuary. Dan Greenwood walked down the aisle in his dark suit. He gestured to a visiting elderly couple where to sit, handed them a bulletin and then promptly walked to the back of the sanctuary again.

Kailey jumped when Dad touched her shoulder and slid in next to her. She stood and walked to the piano as Pastor Liam climbed the three steps to the pulpit. Kailey quickly opened her song book to the opening song of praise and looked across the expanse at the front of the auditorium to smile at Mrs. Berry. The smile was returned and then Pastor Liam began to speak.

"Good morning and welcome to everyone who has gathered to worship this morning. Especially welcome to our visitors. Please stay after the service for refreshments." He looked down at the pulpit and arranged his papers, then his chestnut head popped up and shared a smile of neat white teeth with the congregation before him. Pastor Liam was in his early thirties and this was his first church. His wife, Katrina, sat on the other end of the row her family occupied. They were an attractive couple—both tall and slim with ready smiles and open faces. "Please stand and open your books to number 435, O for a Thousand Tongues to Sing, and we'll join together singing the six verses."

Mrs. Berry played the introduction and then Kailey set her fingers to work, joining the organ and the congregation in the song. After the greeting, singing more songs, reading from the Bible, and prayer, Pastor Liam began his sermon. He was doing a sermon series on the Fruits of the Spirit from Galatians chapter six. He was up to "gentleness" and spoke about how gentleness was connected to having a humble and gracious spirit.

"It's hard to be gentle on the outside when you're angry on the inside. Selfish anger is opposed to God and if we're feeding emotions that are opposed to God, we cannot expect His Spirit to share more of Himself with us. That goes for bitterness, pride, selfish desires, lust, you fill in the blank. Don't expect God to bless you if you refuse to submit your sin to Him. The only way to submit your sin to His authority is with the help of Jesus. Won't you come to Jesus today and tell Him of your shortcomings and ask for forgiveness? He is ready and willing to forgive. All you need to do is ask. Shall we pray?"

Kailey's fingers finished the last notes of the doxology then she stood to exit with the rest of the people. When she reached the doorway to the fellowship hall, she shook Pastor Liam's hand and returned his smile.

"Thank you for playing today, Kailey."

"Thank you for preaching today, Pastor Liam. You put a lot more work into your sermon than I do in my piano playing."

"That may be true, but you're still using your gift to help us worship and we appreciate it. I'm sure God does, too."

"Thanks for the encouragement."

Pastor Liam gently touched her shoulder and then shook the hand of the person behind her. Kailey picked up a cup of tea and then scanned the room for Amanda and Maria. She saw Chelsey sitting beside Mrs. Kennedy with a baby on her lap, talking up a storm. Mrs. Kennedy leaned her gray head down to listen and the baby gurgled happily as Chelsey bounced her. Kailey smiled.

"Who are you smiling at?" Aunt Louise asked, coming up behind her.

"Chelsey. Look at her." Kailey pointed and watched as Aunt Louise's face turned up in a grin of its own.

"She's a pretty special girl."

"She told me this morning I looked like a giant jack-o-lantern."

Aunt Louise turned to her in shock. "Why would she say that? You're wearing black and blue."

"I was wearing black and bright orange."

"Oh, I'm glad you changed." Aunt Louise sipped her tea.

"How have the swimming lessons been going?"

"Good. I have a few students who think they should always be allowed to do some kind of freestyle swim. And some parents who agree."

Kailey rolled her eyes. "That must be fun."

"I'm not sure why they're taking swimming *lessons* if they don't want to learn anything." Aunt Louise sipped her tea again. "But they're the ones paying for it."

"That's true." Kailey poked Edwin, a little boy she used to babysit, as he ran by. He stopped and poked her back before continuing his escapade.

Devin found her a short time later and informed her they were going home for lunch.

"The kids in Sunday school today were very loud," Kailey whispered into the darkness of their bedroom.

"That's the way kids are," Chelsey said.

"But I wasn't very patient with them." Kailey paused. "And I wasn't very patient with you this morning. Sorry, Chelsey."

"I forgive you. I wasn't very kind about saying you looked like a pumpkin. Sorry about that."

"I forgive you."

"Goodnight, Kailey. Love you."

"Love you, too. More than peanut butter cookies."

"More than paintbrushes," Chelsey murmured.

"More than cream on poison ivy."

"More than bug spray in the woods at night."

"More than the piano."

"More than—"

"I love you both more than all those things," came Dad's deep voice from the other side of the door. "Goodnight."

"Goodnight!" both girls yelled back in the darkness. They both heard Dad mutter something as his footsteps sounded down the hall. The girls giggled in the night, and then there was silence.

"Kailey?" Chelsey whispered.

"What?" Kailey moaned in her half-conscious state.

"I love you more than chocolate-chip-peanut-butter cookies."

Kailey smiled beneath her blankets. "Ditto. Goodnight."

CHAPTER SIX

Chelsey left art class on Thursday with her sketchbook under her arm. She waved goodbye to her teacher, Miss Jones, and walked down the hall. Amanda was sick and Kailey and Maria were at volleyball practice. She was going to meet them at the gym and continue to work on her pictures. Then Dad would pick her and Kailey up after practice on his way home from work. She smiled to herself. She was walking alone, *alone*. Her protective big sister wasn't anywhere near her and none of their well-meaning friends were peeking over her shoulder, making sure everything was okay. People were always watching over her. It was like living in jail, a safe jail where the idea was to keep the bad guys out and Chelsey in.

But at this moment she wasn't in jail. She was walking down the hallway at school for the first time without anyone to walk with her. There weren't even any teachers around. She turned the corner and bumped into something solid. She looked up into Bret Wilson's angry eyes.

"Hey retard, watch where you're going."

"Sorry," she whispered and tried to sidestep him but then she bumped into Logan. *This is bad. This is bad. This is bad, bad, bad!*

"Didn't you just hear what he said? Watch where you're going," Logan said and gave her a shove. She spun around and hit another solid object, Todd, who shoved her back toward Bret.

"Get away from me, freak. I don't want whatever you've got."

"No kidding, Todd."

The boys pushed her round and round. Chelsey felt her head swim and her legs begin to throb. She felt her arms bruise as they pushed her from one person to the next. She shut her eyes. *Oh, why was I excited to walk alone? God, will you send someone to help me? Maybe an angel? Well, it doesn't have to be an angel. Just someone big who can save me. And if I die, can you somehow let Kailey know it's not her fault? And Mom and Dad and Devin know that I loved them and—*

"Hey!" a tenor shout interrupted her prayer and the hands that had been shoving her. Chelsey's legs couldn't support her any longer. She collapsed on the floor. From her crumpled position, she heard a voice she didn't recognize. "Leave her alone! What did she do to you?"

"She bumped me," Logan said.

"So you're circle-beating her?"

"Do you want a turn?"

"Chelsey?" Now she thought she heard Amanda. "Move it, dude." She looked up as her friend pushed Jeff out of the way and came to kneel before her. "Chelsey, are you okay?"

She didn't answer. Her eyes were filled with a mix of fear and concern as Logan, Jeff, and Bret pushed past a tall, blond boy she didn't know. They walked down the hallway, laughing, and didn't turn back.

"Chelsey." Amanda's voice made her turn her head. "Are you okay?"

"I don't know," she said. Her voice cracked and her eyes filled with tears. She touched her arm and looked up at her friend. "I didn't mean to make them mad," she whispered.

"Chelsey, you didn't do anything wrong. They were just being mean."

"That's right."

Both girls' heads jerked up to look at the blond boy who stood over them. He cleared his throat. "I'm Mark. Mark Davis. I'm Coach Davis' nephew."

"I'm Amanda McGee and this is Chelsey Martin, and we are very glad to meet you, Mark. You're our hero today."

"Well, you're the one who really made them stop." Mark ducked his head and a slight blush rose to his cheeks.

"Oh yeah." She flexed her arm from where she sat on the floor. "I could have taken them all!"

Chelsey giggled.

Amanda turned to her. "Why are you laughing? I know origami."

"Miss Evens showed us that in World Cultures. It's paper folding."

"So? I bet you could hurt someone with it."

"Maybe if you made a sword," Mark said, joining in.

Chelsey giggled again.

"Think you can stand up and we'll go to the gym? I can leave you there and you can wait for Kailey. I have to run, though, because Mom said we have to go dress shopping for our cousin's wedding." Amanda made a face. "I don't know why we can't just wear the same clothes we normally wear."

"I can take her if you've got to go," Mark said.

"You wouldn't mind?" Amanda asked.

"No, no problem at all. I have to walk down there to meet my uncle anyway. I'll take her," Mark assured her with a smile that could have melted ice.

Amanda stood and turned to Chelsey. "Would you be okay with that, Chelsey?"

"I guess," Chelsey said. *Why is he talking to her like I'm not even here? Does he think I'm dumb? That I don't understand? I don't like him.*

Amanda helped her stand and gave her a hug and then darted down the hallway to the parking lot, her sneakers sounding loudly on the tiled floor.

Chelsey walked beside Mark all the way to the gymnasium. He sat beside her through the entire practice. She ignored him. She frowned. Kailey and Maria kept sending her confused looks from where they stood on the court. She ignored them, too. She didn't want to be friends with this guy. It wasn't her choice that he had come along when he did. It would have been just as good if one of the guys from their church had helped her, like Al Fisher or Dan Greenwood. They were nice and went to her school; they could have helped. But they hadn't. And now she was stuck with this fellow who thought she was dumb and was crowding her space. She sighed heavily and turned away from him.

She waited for Kailey to shower, but as soon as she came out of the change room Chelsey stood and walked toward the door. "Goodbye Mark," was all she said to her hero.

"Bye, see you around," Mark answered.

Kailey looked confused about her sister's rude tone. She waved to the young man who she had bumped into on the first day of school, and then followed Chelsey out the door and into Dad's car. She asked what happened, but Chelsey wouldn't talk. Her lips were zipped tight from where she sat in the back seat, looking out the window. Dad sent a questioning look at Kailey, but she just shrugged. Uncle Bruno's voice came on the radio, giving the traffic report.

Chelsey kept her eyes locked on the passing scenery. She brushed a tear away from her eye so that Dad and Kailey wouldn't see it. *I am not dumb. I am not.*

Mark stirred the pasta and then returned the lid to its original place. Next he moved the wooden spoon to the frying pan simmering with tomato sauce and hamburger. Everything was almost ready. He turned on the oven so the cheese on the garlic bread would melt. The cupboard door opened to reveal dinner plates and tall glasses. He was putting the cutlery on the table when he heard footsteps in the hall and looked up just as his uncle entered wearing track pants and slippers.

"Smells good, Mark," Davis said.

"Thank you. I think we're ready." Mark mixed the noodles and sauce and put the pot on the table, then cut the garlic bread and added it to their spread. Both men sat down and Davis prayed for the meal. Davis served the noodles and Mark passed him the bread.

"So, why was the Martin girl upset with you today?" Davis broke the silence.

"What Martin girl?"

"The one you sat beside through practice and didn't say one thing to."

"I don't think she was upset with *me*. I think she was just upset."

"Why would that be?"

Mark explained what happened and his uncle piled more noodles onto his plate and listened quietly. When he finished, Mark bit his garlic bread.

"I'm glad you stood up for her. I don't think it's easy being either one of those girls. One's got problems and a sister who helps and the other has help and a sister who's got problems," Davis muttered.

"What?" Mark gave him a quizzical look.

"Never mind. I'm sure she was upset about what those boys did, but I also think she was upset with you, too. She kept looking at you and frowning and then turning away."

"That's weird."

"Women are weird. You'll never understand them." Davis stood to refill his glass of water. "But no one ever will. They seem to like being safe and when they don't have to carry stuff. If you protect them and help them, you'll be further ahead than most men. Good supper, Mark. Thank you." Davis clapped him on the back. "I'll do the dishes. You probably have homework. Or call your mom—she'd probably like a report. Tell her I say hello."

Mark left the table and went to his bedroom. Homework first and then he'd call his family once he got stuck. He sat down to Social Studies with the Martin girls still very much in mind.

CHAPTERSEVEN

After dinner, Mom sat in the kitchen with a cup of tea, reading her favourite home magazine. Kailey slid into the office chair by the computer in the kitchen and talked with Maria online. Devin had finally gone to shower after Mom promised they could have popcorn once he was finished. Dad, meanwhile, sat in the living room reading a book that Mom had started earlier but then abandoned when he picked it up.

Chelsey left the safety of her bedroom and came to stand before her father's lazy boy.

"Daddy?"

Dad's balding head bent over the book before him. "Yes, Pumpkin?"

"Can I sit with you?" Her voice was quiet and small.

Dad looked up and put the book down to take his fifteen-year-old daughter onto his lap. Once she was settled, he said, "What's up?"

He heard her sob against his chest. "They are mean to me. And they are mean to Kailey too, because she looks like me."

Dad rubbed her back and waited.

"It's not her fault she looks like me. They say we're stupid. Today I was walking alone down the hall to the gym and I bumped into one of them and he pushed me and then they were all pushing me and I have a bruise on my arm and I didn't know what to do so I started to pray for you—"

"Why were you praying for me?" Dad interrupted.

"For all of you. That you would know I love you even though I'd be dead."

"Chelsey..."

Dad's concerned voice made her sob again. "And then this boy stopped them and Amanda came and helped and the boy talked about me like I wasn't there and then walked me to the gym. I didn't like him."

"The boy who helped you?"

"Yeah, Mark. He thought I was stupid." Chelsey wiped her tears and runny nose with her sweater sleeve. "But Logan is the meanest one ever. He hurt me. And he always calls us names even though we never do anything to him. And," she whispered, "he lives next door."

Dad kept rubbing her back. When he was quite sure she had finished her crying, he spoke. "So what are you going to do?"

"Never go to school again. No school, no Logan, no Mark who thinks I'm dumb, no front steps to go up and down."

"Chelsey," Dad said, his voice deep and serious.

Chelsey didn't answer. She snuggled closer to his chest and waited.

"Chelsey, I think sometimes they call you names and pretend that you aren't there because they don't understand that God made us all differently. Different isn't bad, so long as it's not sin. Red and blue are both good, just different. But honey, you don't need to worry so much about what they do to you. You need to worry about how you respond to them."

"What?" What did he mean? They pushed her and called her names and thought she was dumb. She did worry about what they might do to her.

"When you get to heaven God isn't going to ask you how mean Logan was or how insensitive Mark was. He's going to ask how *you* responded to them. You are responsible for you. So what are you going to do?"

"I don't know."

"What do you think Jesus wants you to do?"

That was *the* worst Dad question ever. Whenever she had a problem and Dad wouldn't tell her what to do, he just said, *What do you think Jesus wants you to do?* And then she had to think and decide on her own.

"He would want me to… to walk around them seven times like the battle of Jericho?" Her voice held hope.

"Do you want to spend forty years in the desert first?"

"No." She sighed, her brow knit in frustration. Dad never let her answer his question the way she wanted to. He always pointed out what was wrong with it until she came up with something that was close to being right. "He wants me to love them the way He loves me. But I don't want to love them," she said with determination. There were many things she could and would do, but loving Logan Stewart was not one of them. That would be like climbing one hundred stairs all by herself.

"Well, do you think Jesus loves you even when you hurt Him?"

She sat up and looked him the eye. "I hurt Jesus?"

"Yes, every time you do something mean or think something bad, you are hurting Jesus." He kissed her forehead.

"Oh, that's a lot. But I don't mean to."

Logan meant to hurt her. Maybe Mark didn't mean it, but she still didn't like him.

"But you still do," Dad said. The good news is that Jesus loves us anyway. He even died for us. He wants us to love other people, because if they believe in Him and ask Him to take away their sins, He'll do it and love them just like He loves you and me."

"So I have to love Logan even though he is mean?" Chelsey's heart fell. This was awful news. She watched the lamp light flicker along the wall. This just wasn't fair. Logan was the one who was mean to her, and had been mean to her for a very long time, and now she was the one who was supposed to be nice? Something was terribly wrong with this situation.

"Yes." Dad's voice made her concentrate again. "That means you have to pray for him and help him understand that God loves you just the way you are. Understand?"

"Oh, I was praying that God would make him move."

"Chelsey."

"Okay, but loving Logan won't be easy."

"And Mark?"

"Both at the same time?"

"Yes."

"Okay, I'll try."

"Let's pray about it right now." With that, Dad bowed his head and prayed for his special girl. When he finished, she gave him a hug.

"Thanks, Daddy. Love you."

"Love you too."

"Popcorn!" Devin bounded down the stairs with his hair still wet from the shower and ran to the kitchen.

"Ready for some popcorn?" Dad asked her.

"Okay, I like popcorn." Chelsey slowly got off his lap, and they went into the kitchen together hand in hand.

CHAPTER EIGHT

Chelsey shivered in her thick green knit sweater and brown corduroys. She stood in the laneway in front of their house, staring up at the maple tree, willing that some of the leaves might fall. The twins had come outside together, but then Kailey had forgotten something and darted back into the house. September was getting chilly. The air smelled fresh and clean with a mix of cut grass and dirt. The tree before Chelsey had allowed some of its green leaves to change into yellows and reds, but it had yet to budge from their summer home.

"But once they do fall," she said to herself, "Devin and I will rake them up into a pile and jump in them." She put her hand over her mouth and giggled at the thought.

Suddenly she heard a noise from the neighbours' house. Logan's house. She turned and saw a very sleepy Logan pull something out of the garage. She heard her father's voice in her head. *Loving people.* Looking up to heaven, she sighed.

"God, I'll go see if he needs help but if he gets mad, You better send an angel or something to come and save me like in the Bible," she proclaimed to the skies and stood still waiting for an answer. The wind blew slightly, teasing the loose hair around her face. She shut her eyes and smiled. She opened them again and with a look of determination walked across the lawn to see what her tangible love-others-as-you-love-yourself lesson was doing.

When she reached his driveway, she saw his mop of brown hair bend over his bike. She stood behind him, got up all her courage and yelled, "Hey! What'cha doing?"

Logan stood and whirled around, pulling up his saggy pants. For a moment words failed him. Where had this girl come from and why was she standing in his garage?

"Do you need any help?"

He blinked and cocked his head to one side. Now he recognized her—the retard girl from school. Why would he want her help? She was helpless, in more ways than one. And where was that bulldog of a sister of hers? He looked around but didn't see her. He turned his attention back to the girl in his garage. Girls never came in his garage.

"What are you doing?" he gave her the angriest look he could muster that early in the morning. Mornings were bad. Nothing good ever happened in the morning. It involved not only emerging from bed but also breakfast. Why everyone got so excited about eating breakfast was beyond him.

"Well, I was looking at our maple tree and I saw you and I thought you might need some help...Do you?"

"No, go away." What did the maple tree have to do with breakfast or helping him?

"Are you sure? Because I will help you if you need me to." She took a step closer and looked at his bike.

"Go away!" Logan pushed her. The force caused her to step backward and lose her balance, but she caught herself before she fell on the pavement. He didn't care. She shouldn't have come over here to begin with. Girls didn't belong in his garage. She was the one who obviously needed help, not him. Besides, she probably didn't know anything about bikes anyway. Why did her parents even let her out of the house? *So they can have some freedom, stupid.*

"Hey!"

Logan looked up. *Oh, there's the bulldog sister.*

"What are you doing?"

Logan stood extra tall as the spitfire redhead marched toward him, sure that his extra six inches would intimidate her.

"Don't push my sister!" She came to stand before him. "Don't even touch her!"

"She's the one who came over here from who knows where and invaded private property."

"We live right next door!" The second sister pointed to the yellow house across the grass.

They did? How did he not know that? He only ever saw them climb the hill and then get off the bus. He never concerned himself with where they lived or what they did.

"Oh," he said, and looked down at the girl before him. She reminded him of the mother bear he'd seen on a documentary the week before. He took a step back, remembering what happened to the bear that got between the mama and her cub. "Well, maybe you should keep her on your side of the grass."

"Kailey, we're going to be late."

The second girl ignored her sister and glared at him again. "Stay away from my sister." Then she turned and picked up the backpack and book bag she had dropped. He watched her take her sister's hand and lead her back up the driveway and then start their assent to the top of the hill. He looked down at his watch. The bus wasn't due for another twenty minutes. He could make it to the top of the hill in two minutes on his bike.

He shrugged and turned back to his task at hand—fixing the chain on his bike. He shook his head. "That girl gets up twenty minutes early just so she can help her stupid sister up the hill. What an idiot!" he muttered to himself.

Friday was volleyball night and the Benton Bears were home to the Canfield Giants. Chelsey took her place behind the home bench and clutched her homemade flag. Devin sat beside her. She turned and waved to Mom and Dad, who were sitting a few rows back talking to Maria's parents.

"Do you have any candy?" she asked Devin.

"No, but you can have half a piece of gum. It's my last one."

"Okay, thanks." She held out her hand as Devin bit his stick of gum in half and handed her the rest. She popped it in her mouth and chewed.

Yellow fruit flavour, her favourite. She turned and looked at her little brother. "You know what?"

"What?"

"You're my favourite little brother."

He looked at her with a puzzled expression on his face. "I'm your only little brother."

"Oh yeah."

Just then the teams ran onto the court. Chelsey screamed wildly and waved her flag.

Devin clapped.

The referee blew his whistle and the game began. The gym filled with the smell of sweat and the sound of screaming. It was a close game. Kailey made a few points and blocked some hard spikes. Maria set her up and she spiked hard on the other team. Chelsey screamed wildly. The teams switched sides. Kailey set to Maria and Maria spiked it. Chelsey heard Mrs. Berry scream.

"You know what?"

"What, Devin?"

He looked at his sister. "You wouldn't think Mrs. Berry was a screamer. I mean, to look at her. She always seems so prim and proper. Last time we were there she made me clean my feet after being on the deck."

"I guess." Chelsey shrugged. Kailey blocked a spike from the other team. Chelsey cheered. The game ended 21–19 for home. Kailey was ecstatic during the car ride home. Dad encouraged her chatter by pointing out all the things she did right on the court.

Chelsey sighed from the back seat.

"What, Chelsey?" Mom called from the front passenger seat.

"All Kailey does is play volleyball, and when she isn't playing it she's talking about it. Can we just do something *normal?*"

"I'll watch a movie with you when we get home," Kailey offered.

"No you won't," Mom said.

"But Mom, it's Saturday tomorrow," Kailey said.

"Yeah, Mom!" Devin chimed in.

Mom and Dad exchanged a look. "Okay, a short one."

At home, Devin put in a western and sat on the couch with his sisters. Kailey sat in the middle. As the movie continued, the space on the couch slowly got smaller and smaller. Soon they were all very snug with a blanket over all three of them and their bodies pressed together like lumber in a clamp. Chelsey woke up to Kailey nudging her gently and telling her it was time for bed.

"Where's Devin?" Chelsey asked sleepily.

"I already helped him upstairs. Come on, pretty lady." Kailey helped her up. They skipped brushing their teeth. Chelsey crawled into bed and muttered a "goodnight" before falling back asleep.

CHAPTER NINE

Kailey walked into English class on Monday morning with a slight headache. She dropped her bag beside her chair and looked over at Mazie. A Kleenex box sat on the top of her desk.

"You feeling okay, Mazie?" She opened her notepad and slid into her seat.

Mazie turned to her. When Kailey looked up, she bit her lip to keep in her gasp. Mazie's nose was red from blowing it too much and big bags sagged under her eyes. "No. Do I look like I'm okay?" She pointed to the black bandana on her head and reached for a tissue. Black bandana days were not good days.

"It sucks that you're sick," Kailey said, avoiding the question.

Mazie blew her nose loudly and a boy turned in his desk two rows ahead and sent her a look of disgust. Mazie blew her nose again. "I feel like I just got run over by a transport truck that made me flat as a pancake, then I got picked up by the wind and stuck to a hydro pole and peed on by some fat kid's dog."

"Did you take any meds?"

"Good morning, class." Both girls looked up as Mr. Marksdale entered the room. He wore a brown striped suit and a large grin that made his round glasses slide up the bridge of his nose. "I hope you all read over the assignment I gave you on Friday."

Logan sauntered in with the usual gloomy expression on his face.

"Mr. Stewart, how good of you to join us. I'm sure you have a good reason for being late, again." Mr. Marksdale stood behind his desk and waited for an answer, but Logan's only response was a shrug as he took his seat behind Kailey. Kailey shivered.

Suddenly Mazie turned to Kailey to whisper something and let out sneeze that shook her seat.

Kailey opened her mouth to scream but no sound came out. She shut her mouth and her eyes bulged open in horror. Mazie's snot was on her arm. "Ew, eww!" She looked up at Mr. Marskdale with round eyes. "May I be excused? I have someone else's snot on my arm."

He nodded. "Mazie, please go with her and clean yourself up."

Kailey led the way out of the room. "Ew, ew, ew."

"Sorry, Kailey." Mazie sniffed.

"It's okay. *Ew!*" Kailey led the way to the bathroom. She quickly turned on the hot water upon entering and started pumping the soap dispenser. Mazie pulled a Kleenex out of its box and blew her nose loudly.

"I should have just stayed home," she muttered, throwing the tissue out and grabbing another.

"Or not talk to people when you have to sneeze," Kailey muttered.

"I said I was sorry."

Kailey took a wad of paper towel to dry her arm. "I know. Sorry for getting mad. I think you should go to the nurse and see if she has anything to help you."

"Okay. Tell Mr. Marskdale for me?"

"Sure." Kailey threw the paper towel in the garbage and headed for the door. Mazie stood thinking and then picked up the Kleenex box and followed her. They parted ways in the hallway so Kailey could go back to class and Mazie could find some decongestants.

"She really snotted on your arm?"

"Devin, that's not polite." Mom frowned at him from across the dinner table.

"Yes Devin, she really sneezed on my arm. It was nasty."

"Did anything come out of her hair?" Chelsey asked.

"Her hair?" Uncle Bruno asked.

"If you ever saw Mazie, you would understand," Kailey said.

"She has lots of stuff sticking out of her hair. It's like having your pencil case on top of your head. I even saw a ruler in there once," Chelsey said.

"Did she get it on anyone else?" Devin asked.

"Devin!"

"I don't think so, but I'm pretty sure Rachel Willis just about hurled."

"Could we change the topic?" Aunt Louise asked. She was looking a little green herself.

"Of course," said Uncle Bruno. "At the station today, Mr. Dale almost had a cow because Andy suddenly had a bloody nose while he was on air and he—"

"Excuse me," Aunt Louise said, and ran to the bathroom.

"Anyway, he almost got blood on some of the equipment."

"Bruno!"

"Oh, sorry Cindy." Uncle Bruno tried to look apologetic as he met his sister-in-law's glare.

The children glanced at each other with questioning eyes. Aunt Louise never threw up. Devin shrugged and went back to his potatoes, and Chelsey spooned more apple sauce into her mouth. Kailey tried to catch Mom's eye, but Mom wouldn't comply.

Aunt Louise came back to a silent dinner table.

"Oh hey, honey. You look great," Uncle Bruno said.

Aunt Louise frowned. "Why don't you just tell them, Bruno."

Kailey looked at Uncle Bruno. He stood and put his arm around his tiny wife. With a grin and a twinkle in his eye, he took a deep breath. "We're gonna have a baby!"

The children sat in silence and then the full meaning of what Uncle Bruno had said struck them and they jumped up and screamed and hugged Aunt Louise and Uncle Bruno and soon everyone was talking all at the same time. Dad quieted them down and they took their seats again.

"Really? Really? I'm going to be an aunt!" Chelsey glowed.

"You're going to have a new cousin, just like how Joel and Andrianna are our cousins," Kailey explained.

Chelsey's glow faded but then it brightened again. "Well cousins are good too! Hurray!"

"When are you due?" Kailey asked.

"May 10," Aunt Louise said.

"Cool. Really cool!"

"So is my beef," Devin muttered.

"Sorry Dev," Aunt Louise said, and rubbed his back. "But cold beef is better than no beef."

"Or losing your beef," Uncle Bruno offered. Aunt Louise frowned at him again. "What?"

"Thanks, dear. That makes me feel so much better."

"What? I'm just saying. At least Cindy is a good cook and the beef is good and we're all enjoying it. Oh, except you, honey."

"Uncle Bruno!" Kailey kicked him under the table.

Uncle Bruno smiled at his little wife. "Shall I get you some crackers?"

"Maybe it will be twins," Devin said, shoveling more potatoes into his mouth.

"No," said Aunt Louise firmly. "Unless they're twin girls."

"I already told you we're only having boys." Uncle Bruno stood and went to the cupboard.

"Well, I forgot to mention it, but I've been praying to have only girls."

Uncle Bruno choked. "You what?" He turned and glared at her, and she pretended to frown back, but her eyes still shone. He walked back and kissed her soundly. The children gagged. Dad stood to get the Bible off the corner shelf and kissed Mom on his way. The children gagged again and wouldn't stop making noises until he returned and opened the book. He was about to read when Aunt Louise stood and ran to the bathroom again. She returned shortly and Dad read. Kailey helped Mom with the dishes and then the ladies sat down to a cup of mint tea while the men when to play in the yard.

CHAPTER TEN

Kailey slipped out of her house an hour before dinner and ran down the street. Periodically Dad would join her, but tonight she wanted to run alone. The sun was making its way to bed behind the clouds and pine trees. Red and yellow streaks lit up the sky, declaring its departure for the next few hours. Kailey smiled. *The heavens declare the glory of God and the skies proclaim His handiwork. Wow, Lord, you sure know how to make your presence known. If I were you, I would be so sick of people seeing it and choosing to ignore you that I would probably bring this whole world to an end. Thanks for putting up with us.*

She turned the corner as Mr. Smee flipped the OPEN sign to CLOSED. She waved at the old man. He returned the wave and sent a holey grin back at her. She continued on her way and passed Apple Lane, the road Uncle Bruno and Aunt Louise lived down. Uncle Bruno and Aunt Louise were going to have a baby. A baby! She smiled. They both looked so happy; well, Uncle Bruno did, Aunt Louise looked happy when she wasn't sick or tired, which left a very small time gap.

The wind blew, sharing the scent of fresh cut grass it had just stolen from Mr. Cho's lawn. Kailey rounded the corner. Volleyball was going well. She and Maria were both flourishing on the team and they had won most of their games. The practices required a lot of dedication, but Coach Davis was a good coach so that made it better; and the fact that a certain nephew of his frequently came to watch their practices while he waited for his uncle wasn't exactly a disappointment either. The fact that Chelsey ignored him was a little disheartening.

Chelsey. Kailey sighed. They would never have a normal conversation about boys or clothes or the prissy girls at school. Chelsey wouldn't listen. She didn't like any boys except for Maria's brothers, and they were all away for school. She didn't care about clothes or bother with prissy girls at school. *Lord, sometimes I get sick of standing up for Chelsey. Please help me to be calm and patient with her. You know how hard it can be to deal with people; you put up with 12 ornery, selfish disciples. Thank you for only giving me one sweet, ornery sister.*

She looked down as she came up to the park. Her shoe was untied. "Well, don't want to trip and fall," she muttered to herself and bent down to knot her lances. She glanced across the park. A lady was pushing a stroller, an elderly man walked slowly holding the hand of a little girl, and a teenage boy was throwing a stick for his Irish Terrier. The dog caught the stick in mid-air and trotted back to his owner. She gasped when the boy turned to throw the stick again and she saw his face. Logan Stewart bent to retrieve the dog's prize and then patted the dog's head with a small smile playing on his lips. He stood and threw the stick again.

Kailey had never seen Logan smile or play with that dog. She had thought it was his mom's. The little dog was cute and he obviously loved his owner, which surprised her almost as much as Logan's smile. Kailey stood and watched them a moment longer before her watch beeped and she began her run again so that she wouldn't be too late for supper. *You're full of surprises, aren't you, God?* She shook her head as she ran home.

"What are you going to do for Thanksgiving on Monday?" Kailey asked Maria from where the girls sat on the Martin's living room floor. A ball of yarn sat on either side of them with two balls between them. Their fingers worked quickly as their crochet hooks dodged and grabbed *in and out, in and out.*

"Terrence, Colin, and Rob are coming home," Maria answered. "Can you pass the scissors?"

"Are you switching colours?"

Maria snipped the blue end and set to work with the deep gray. "Yup, my mom wants a striped scarf for Christmas and these are her favourite colours."

Chelsey chose that moment to walk through to the kitchen. She nearly tripped on them with their backs against the wall of the staircase and their legs stretched out on the living room rug.

"Why are you sitting here?" Chelsey asked with a furrowed brow.

"The floor is a cool place to be," Kailey answered.

Chelsey wrinkled her nose and continued to the kitchen.

"Hey, Chelsey, my brothers are coming home for Thanksgiving," Maria said.

She stopped and wheeled around, excitement dancing in her blue eyes. "Really? They really are? Will they play games with me?"

"I think Mom was going to ask if your family wanted to come over on Saturday for a while."

"Yes!" Chelsey clapped her hands in delight and hurried to the kitchen to share the good news with Mom.

"She really likes your brothers."

"I guess."

"No, really. They're the only guys that she likes other than Devin." Kailey stood and rubbed her behind. "I'm going numb. Want to go for a walk before your dad comes to get you?"

"Okay, just let me finish this row."

The girls wrapped up their loose threads and put them away in their baskets and bags and then found their sneakers. The weather had turned a bit cool with the change into October. Canadian Thanksgiving is always celebrated on the second Monday of October, which meant Maria's brothers would be home in just under a week. When the girls returned from their walk, they found their mothers talking. Mrs. Berry did indeed invite the Martins to come over the following Saturday for the afternoon and dinner.

CHAPTER ELEVEN

When Chelsey heard about the invitation, she could hardly contain her excitement. She danced in the kitchen and asked Kailey to play the piano so she could dance again in the living room. She told Amanda on Sunday at youth group, and had a smile plastered on her face throughout the week. She even smiled at Mark when he came to youth group Bible study on Wednesday night with Al and Dan.

On Saturday, she woke up early and stood smiling at Kailey until her twin opened her eyes on the top bunk.

"Yah!" Kailey screamed and rolled over.

"Kailey! Today is the day!"

"The day for what? Scaring your sister so bad she wets her pants?"

"The day we get to see the brothers!" Chelsey jumped a little and slipped on the wood floor in her socks. She grabbed the bunk bed to steady herself.

"We aren't going there till 2:30 this afternoon," Kailey said.

"It doesn't matter! Today is the day! Will you get up?"

Kailey pulled the blankets off her and reached for her rob. "Yes, because you frightened me so bad when I first woke up and now you keep shaking the bed, so I have to go to the bathroom or I'll wet myself." She pulled on her slippers and ran out the door.

Chelsey followed her out of their room and sat beside Devin on the couch, where he was watching cartoons.

"Why are the best cartoons always on before 7:00 am?" Devin asked.

"I don't know." Chelsey shrugged. A few moments later a movement caught her eye. "Kailey, come watch with us!"

Kailey frowned at her. "It's Saturday. I want to go back to bed."

"This one is your favourite. It's with the mice that talk and travel all over the world," Devin said. Both he and Chelsey looked at Kailey with hope-filled eyes.

"Okay, okay, I'm coming." Kailey smooshed onto the couch beside Chelsey and there the three of them sat until Mom and Dad got up two hours later. After breakfast, Dad set them all to work in the yard, picking up twigs and pulling weeds so he could mow the lawn.

Chelsey picked up a stick from the yard. *I don't want to carry this all the way to the wheelbarrow.* She quickly looked around and then threw the stick over the fence. A dog barked. Chelsey jumped. She crouched down and looked through the space in the fence. A little dog stood staring back at her with the stick in his mouth.

"Hello, doggie. I would play with you if I could, but I have to help clean up the yard."

"Chelsey!"

"See what I mean? If I find another good stick, I'll throw it for you," she whispered and the dog barked back at her and ran away.

After the children were done outside, Mom set them to work inside. They bartered off the bad jobs, like dusting and cleaning the bathroom, and soon the house shone. Mom made cinnamon buns and chili for lunch, and then they changed out of their work clothes and packed themselves into the van to go to the Berrys' house.

The Berrys lived across town in a white, two-story house with a white fence to match. Mr. Berry owned his own cleaning company, and now that their children were older, Mrs. Berry did the bookwork for the company and taught a handful of organ students. Chelsey took Dad's hands to help her up the steps to their porch and Kailey opened the door to let them all in while calling a greeting to the household to announce their arrival. The house smelled like fresh bread and turkey.

Maria and Mr. Berry came to the door to welcome them.

"Where are the boys?" Chelsey asked.

"Boys?" Mr. Berry asked with a quizzical brow.

"Aren't they here?" Chelsey asked, looking distressed.

Maria laughed. "Don't mind him, he's just being a pest. Terry, Colin, and Rob are all here. They heard you drive up and decided to start the day off right with a game of hide and seek. Good luck finding them. I think they're in the backyard."

"Let's go!" Devin picked up his shoes and darted down the hallway to the backyard. Chelsey was close on his heels. Devin helped her put on her shoes and climb down the stairs at the back of the house. The Berrys' house backed onto a woods with trails. Chelsey and Devin started their search in the main yard itself, and then scampered into the woods.

"Devin, we are never going to find them," Chelsey said after they had been searching for fifteen minutes.

"Yes we will," Devin said. "They can only hide for so long until they get bored."

"That's what you think!"

Chelsey and Devin froze. "Colin!" They ran toward the sound of the voice but couldn't find anyone. Just then a pinecone landed a few inches away from Devin's foot. He frowned at Chelsey.

"What? I didn't throw that at you."

"Then where'd it come from?"

This time a pinecone hit his shoulder.

Both children looked up to see the three Berry brothers sitting in the tree above their heads, smirking.

"Hey!" Devin yelled. "I thought climbing trees was against the rules."

"Since when?" Terrence, Colin, and Rob all climbed down to meet them on the ground.

"I can't climb trees," Chelsey said.

"Well then, we won't climb trees for the rest of the game," Terrence said, and gave her a hug. Terrence was the oldest of the Berry children. He was studying law and lived in Toronto. Next came Colin, who also gave Chelsey a hug. He was working on his BA in Biology and Chemistry in Ottawa. Last of all, Rob came forward to embrace her. Rob was away for his first year after high school and was taking a general year of study in Hamilton before deciding what he wanted to do. All three boys were tall with wavy brown hair and dark eyes that were always laughing.

The party went to the backyard to establish boundaries and decide who was *it* next when Kailey and Maria came out to join them. They played hide and seek for an hour, and then the dads came out with a soccer ball and hide and seek was forgotten.

"We should be playing football for Thanksgiving," Colin said.

"We could play tackle soccer," Devin suggested.

The eyes of all the men lit up. The teams were chosen. Terrence, Colin, Mr. Martin, and Kailey against Rob, Maria, Mr. Berry, Devin, and Chelsey. They made the nets with some chunks of wood from the forest and the game was on. Terrence ran with the ball and Devin jumped on him. The ball was passed to Mr. Martin, who was hip-checked by Mr. Berry, and then Kailey had the ball and took off across the lawn.

"Get her! Get her!" Devin screamed, still on Terrence's shoulders, bouncing down the field.

"I'll get her," Maria called back, but she couldn't run as fast Kailey.

Kailey made for the net, which Rob was dutifully guarding. She saw a spark light his eye and for a split second wondered if a wiser course could be taken. Rob didn't let her think long. He ran out of the net and with little effort picked her five-foot-four-inch frame up, threw her over his shoulder, and kicked the ball to his father.

"Let me down!" Kailey shrieked.

Chelsey stood on the sidelines laughing.

Rob ignored her pleas and ran down the field with his father till they scored on the opposite net. Devin let out a yell of triumph. Rob placed a very red Kailey on the ground.

"Not legal! This is tackle soccer, not 'commandeer the opposite team's players' soccer!" Kailey's green eyes shone from the fresh air and exercise. She tried to glare at Rob, but he just laughed.

"If I had tackled you, you would have died. I'm a bit taller than you."

"Whatever."

Maria jogged up and took the ball. "Only like an entire foot, Rob, and you probably weigh like a hundred pounds more than her. No big deal. You can take him, Kailey."

"I'll help you!" Devin shouted from behind Rob and jumped on his back.

"He's got me!" Rob winked at Kailey and started running down the field toward his own end with Devin hanging on for dear life.

The dinner was delicious. Mom and Mrs. Berry had made scalloped potatoes, turkey, salad, green beans, corn, stuffing, gravy, and cranberry sauce. They drank wine and ate apple pie and all declared they were too full to run any more. After dinner, Maria loaded the dishwasher and then showed Devin and Chelsey her lizards. Colin and Kailey washed and dried the pots and pans, and Rob and Terrence wiped the counters and table and put everything away. Then they all retired to the living room for an hour before the Martins departed.

Thanksgiving came and went for Logan. He hadn't thought much about it except that his mom made stuffing from a box, Mitch was over for the long weekend, and he didn't go to school. He spent the Monday at home. He peeled potatoes for his Mom and then took Nog for a walk. Their lunch was a quiet affair, since Mom's parents had died a couple years before and Dad's parents wouldn't be coming. *Of course not.*

Logan rode his bike to Lori's to spend the evening with her family. Lori was cute. Her face held two deep blue gems and a nose that turned up at the end, spotted with a few freckles, and her red mouth finished off the work of art. That mouth. He felt a small spark of warmth in his core. Very possibly the best thing he had discovered about that girl so far was her mouth.

He parked his bike in their garage and then went inside. Her little sisters met him at the door with pictures and homemade artwork to display. Lori thought they were cute, so he nodded his head and pretended to pay attention while they put on their show. They showed him something new every time he came. At least that's what they said—it all looked like the same trash to him. He slid past her sisters and walked toward the kitchen. Her brothers were sitting in the den watching football, sometimes cheering and sometimes swearing. Logan avoided them even more than he avoided the little girls. Lori's older brothers creeped him out. They were a little weird—not the cool, dress-a-bit-different-than-everyone-else type of weird, more like I-can't-put-my-finger-on-what's-wrong-with-you weird.

Lori stood with her mom in the kitchen. "Happy Thanksgiving," Mrs. White said.

Lori looked up and gave him *that* smile. "Hey, good lookin'," she said, taking his hand before turning to her mother. "We have a few minutes before dinner is ready, right Mom?"

Mrs. White nodded. She looked tired. She always looked tired.

Lori took his hand and led him to the living room. She sat on the couch. He sat next to her. "What are you thankful for this year, Logan?"

Her voice was sweet syrup in his ears. "I don't think there is anything to be thankful for," he said.

She leaned over and kissed him soundly. He kissed her back. Her hands moved to the sides of his face and his wrapped around her back. She suddenly pulled back slightly and whispered, "Still can't think of anything to be thankful for?"

"Kiss me again and I'll keep thinking," he answered and kissed her again.

When Logan got home, he was in a foul mood. He and Lori had been in the middle of their make-out session when her brother called them for dinner. He jumped off his bike, dropped it on the garage floor and went inside, closing the door with a resounding *slam* behind him. Dinner had been bad. Not the food, the food had been very good. The company had been bad. Her brothers made crude jokes about everyone at the table, her dad sat at the head of the table and didn't say anything except to periodically get up and yell at the dog, and her sister continually kicked him under the table.

Footsteps sounded behind him but he didn't turn to see who it was. Growling under his breath, he continued to search the fridge.

"How was Lori's house?" Mom asked.

"Awful," he replied. "Where's the milk?"

"We're all out," she said quietly. "I'll get more tomorrow. I'll make some popcorn right now if you take out the garbage."

He turned and shut the fridge door with a bang. Mom jumped a little, but she met his gaze and held it firmly. Their eyes locked and in that moment they both seemed understand: neither had had a joyful Thanksgiving. Logan reached under the sink and pulled out the garbage and headed out the back door. His mother padded her back on the way to the back door.

The night air was crisp. "This is stupid. What a dumb holiday! *Thanksgiving,*" he snorted. "As if I have anything to be thankful for." He lifted the lid of the dumpster.

"Happy Thanksgiving, Logan."

He whirled around to see where the quiet voice had come from. One of the Martin girls stood a few feet away on her side of the fence, holding a cat. The calico obviously loved her owner because she was nuzzling up against her chin. It purred loudly and would have grinned if it knew how.

"Hi," he muttered and lifted his hand in some sort of wimpy wave, feeling rather awkward but not knowing what else to do.

She looked into the night sky. "What are you thankful for, Logan?" she asked in a tone of awe as she looked at the stars.

"Nothing." He dumped the garbage into the dumpster.

Her head snapped around. "Well that is real dumb."

He shrugged.

"There is *so* much to be thankful for! Like our families and friends and chocolate and animals and everything else God has given us."

"Well, there is no such thing as God, but if there was He sure hasn't given me anything. It's more like He just takes stuff." Logan dusted off his hands and turned to go inside. "Crazy chick," he muttered under his breath.

"Well, God made the stars and they're pretty cool. I mean when you think about it. And God made you. It's pretty amazing, really; God thought up making so many people and they are all different. Maybe you just have to look harder to see those things," she called after him. "God doesn't make mistakes, Logan. Happy Thanksgiving!"

He shook his head as he walked inside. *Even if there was a God, what have I got to be thankful for? What's a family without a father? And friends? I don't even know what a true friend is. Nope, God's done nothing for me.*

"Did you know that Logan doesn't believe in God?" Chelsey whispered in the dark.

"I never suspected that he did," Kailey replied.

"Oh."

"Why?"

"I just thought everyone at least believed in God, even if they don't love Jesus."

"Oh."

Both girls lay in silence, deep in their own thoughts. Their hair smelled like the hairspray Kailey had used in the morning getting ready for the Thanksgiving service at church. This time she wore the orange skirt with a white top and blue sweater. It even obtained Chelsey's approval.

"Kailey?"

"Yeah, Chelsey?"

"Will you pray that Logan can think of something to be thankful for?"

"Chelsey, don't be weird."

"I'm serious," she said a little too loudly.

"Shh…okay, I'll pray that he can be thankful for something. Goodnight."

"Goodnight."

Kailey rolled over and pulled her blanket up to her chin.

"Kailey?"

Kailey grunted in reply.

"I love you more than *not* having squash for supper."

"I love you more than Canadian pizza," Kailey replied sleepily.

"I love you more than the sunset."

"I love you more than orange juice for breakfast."

"I love you more than comfy shoes."

"I love you more than weekends with no homework."

"I love you more than the colour blue."

"I love you more than running."

"That's a lot. Goodnight, Kailey."

"Goodnight, Chelsey."

CHAPTER TWELVE

"She's sitting by the window, reading a book."

Mark's head snapped around and he met Al Fisher's eyes. Al was slightly shorter than Mark with brown hair that desperately needed to be introduced to a scissor. Mark thought Al had blue eyes, but he couldn't be sure until his hair actually met the scissor. They had met shortly after Mark moved in with his uncle. Al lived four houses down and went to the same church as Coach Davis. Al and his friend, Dan Greenwood, has seen it as their duty to show Mark his way around and in the process became his friends.

"Pardon?" Mark stuck his chin out.

Al smiled and poked Dan. "Dan, who's sitting by the window with a book?"

Dan, a tall blond fellow with a great appreciation for plaid, nonchalantly glanced up. "Oh, that's Kailey Martin."

"Yeah, her. Mark, why don't you just ask her out on a date and stop walking around like a sick puppy dog?"

"Because he isn't old enough to drive, so they'd have to go on his bicycle," Dan snorted. "Maybe Mark can pedal and Kailey can sit in the basket."

"Stop it, guys. I don't even like her."

"Really?" said Al. "Then why did you just put mustard on our carrots?"

Mark looked down at his plate and groaned.

"I'm telling you, just ask her out. You'll start eating a lot better." Al laughed and slapped him on the back.

"Or maybe you'll start a new food company and become rich," Dan said.

Mark groaned again.

Kailey arrived at English class early on Wednesday morning. Mr. Marksdale was already there writing on the blackboard. She smiled at her teacher and then took her seat. She was digging through her bag when his voice caused her to look up.

"Ms. Martin?"

"Yes, Mr. Marksdale?"

He walked up and took a seat on the top of the desk across from her. "Ms. Martin, is everything alright?"

"Yes." Kailey's face filled with concern.

"I only ask because usually you're later because you have to take your sister to her class first. Is she alright?"

Kailey pulled her hair behind her ear and smiled a small, bashful smile. "She's fine. Our friend is walking with her this morning. Thanks for asking." Kailey turned her attention back to the contents of her bag, but looked up again when she sensed that her teacher hadn't moved.

"Pardon me, Ms. Martin, but how are *you?*"

She blinked. How was she? Why was did he care? She didn't even like his class. "I'm fine," she said with a nod.

Mr. Marksdale's brown eyes locked with her green ones and didn't move for a moment. She didn't know what he was searching for, but he must have found the answer to his question because he smiled and walked back to the blackboard.

"Amanda?"

"What's up, cute duck?" Amanda answered, blowing a bubble.

"What do you want to do once you're done high school?" Kailey asked.

"I don't know. Maybe work at the burger joint for a while."

"I was being serious." Kailey looked across the McGees' backyard. Canadian Geese flew overhead in a V formation, calling to one another.

"So was I. I like making burgers."

"I don't think that's your calling."

"Well, I guess we'll find out. Why? What do you want to do?" Amanda picked up a fallen leaf and twirled it between her fingers.

"I don't know. Do you have any ideas?"

"You can always work at the burger joint with me."

"Wow, thanks, you're a true friend." Kailey rolled her eyes.

"I don't think you need to freak out about this. God will show you what you should do, when you should do it. I mean, you know what you need to do tomorrow, so why worry about what you need to do in four years? Start praying about it and see what God says."

Kailey studied her friend for a long time.

"What?" Amanda touched her hair. "Do I have something in my teeth?"

"That might be the wisest thing I've ever heard you say."

"Really? I need to say wise stuff more often."

The friends sat in silence for a few moments, left alone with their own thoughts. Kailey pulled her sweater closer around her slim body and took a deep breath. After school, Mom had picked up Chelsey and brought her home, and Kailey had gone to Amanda's until youth group that night. Youth group was becoming unpleasant. She thought Mark Davis was a nice enough fellow, even cute, possible boyfriend material, but he watched her *all the time*. It was an unnerving thing to be watched by a member of the opposite sex that she didn't know very well. Chelsey didn't like Mark at all. That much was clear. She refused to greet him and spent almost as much time glaring at him as he did watching Kailey. She sighed.

"Mr. Marksdale talked to me today. He asked how I was," Kailey said quietly.

Amanda looked at her. "What did you say?"

Kailey shrugged. "I said I was fine."

"Is that true?"

Kailey met her friend's eyes and for the second time that day she felt her soul being searched. "I think so."

Amanda waited and slid over on the grass and gave her a hug. "I love you, Kailey Martin."

"I love you, too, Amanda McGee. I'm glad you're my friend." Kailey hugged her back. The girls let go and looked at each other again. "Not only because you're so amazing, but also because your mother is an exceptional cook."

Amanda grinned. "Well then, I say we go find out what she's been cooking!"

They stood and ran into the warm house. Smells of fresh cookies and a casserole in the oven and Handel's *Messiah* greeted them. They both took a handful of cookies and retired to the basement to play video games until dinner.

That Sunday, Kailey taught Sunday school. She loved the three-year-olds, from their prayer requests (Lewis' cat had a cold and Tammy had a new swing) to their questions: Did Jesus ever sneeze? Did Asaph lead music with a guitar or an organ? What would have happened if one of Noah's sons was allergic to cats? Kailey answered their questions to the best of her abilities, but when it came to the ones she didn't know, she instructed them to ask their parents when they got home.

"How was Sunday school today?" Mom asked from the front seat as Dad drove the van home that evening after the second service.

"Most of them were good. Calvin put play dough in the carpet and when I asked him if he thought it was okay, he said they always do it at home."

"I bet they do," Dad said.

Kailey's head bobbed back and forth as Dad drove. She breathed onto the window and then drew a picture on the steamed glass. The van thermometer said it was only 4°C. The streetlights flickered overhead.

"It feels like Christmas," Chelsey chimed from the back seat.

"We just had Thanksgiving!" Devin objected, poking her. Chelsey squawked in reply.

Dad parked in the driveway. Kailey helped Chelsey up the steps while Dad unlocked the front door. She flipped off her shoes and ran to the kitchen.

"I'll make the hot chocolate," she called over her shoulder while the rest of the family went to change out of their Sunday clothes.

Sunday nights, the Martin family had a free-for-all supper and Dad read to them. She was still smiling to herself about Calvin and the play dough episode when her right foot made contact with the kitchen floor and swept out from under her.

Kailey screamed.

She hit the floor with a *thud*. Pain shot from her ankle up the rest of her leg. She closed her eyes and screamed again.

"What are you doing?"

She heard Devin run to the doorway and stop.

"Dad? Dad!"

Kailey moaned, holding her leg. "Dad!"

"What's going on?" Dad ran up to the kitchen.

Kailey opened her eyes and looked up at his white face. She followed his eyes to her leg that was lying in a dangerously acute angle. She bit her lip to keep from screaming, but tears streamed out her eyes and made rivers down her face. "It hurts!" she cried, looking up at Dad again.

Mom stood in the doorway and Dad knelt on the floor beside Kailey. "I waxed it yesterday," she whispered.

"Better call the hospital." Dad looked at Mom before bringing his attention back to Kailey. "The paramedics will be here in no time, honey, don't worry."

Kailey nodded. "Can you pack me track pants and a hoodie, Mom?" she asked, still in her skirt and blouse from church.

"Right away." Mom walked away with the phone in her hand, dialing the hospital on her way to the twins' room.

"Do you think it's broken?" Kailey asked.

Dad smiled. "Well, I am only an electrician, but I'm pretty confident the answer to that question is yes."

Tears were still pouring out of Kailey's eyes.

"Don't be upset, Kailey," Devin said, sitting on the floor next to her and taking her hand. "I'll sign your cast and I won't even write anything dumb on it."

"Thanks, Dev," Kailey said, offering a small smile through her tears.

Mom came back with a T-shirt and zip-up hoodie. Devi and Dad left the room while Mom helped Kailey slip out of her blouse and pull on something more comfortable. Kailey was just doing up the zipper when she heard sirens. A few minutes later, two paramedics followed Dad into the kitchen with a stretcher. They positioned Kailey on it and strapped her down for the ride to the hospital.

"Dad?" Kailey looked at him with frightened eyes.

"I'll go with you in the ambulance," Dad said.

Chelsey stood beside the stairs as the paramedics took Kailey out the door on a stretcher. "Love you more than gingerbread men at Christmas, Kailey. Don't die."

Kailey sent her sister a brave smile. "Love you more than no flies in the summer. I will do my utmost not to die." She gritted her teeth and closed her eyes.

"Dad?" Kailey asked inside the ambulance. One of the paramedics, a middle-aged man with graying hair and sharp blue eyes, was sitting beside her father to her left. The other medic was driving.

"Yeah, kiddo?"

"How will we get home?"

"Hitchhike," Dad said.

The medic beside him started to smile.

"I think that's illegal," Kailey said.

"Okay, then I'll call Uncle Bruno and have him pick us up. He doesn't have to work till eleven tomorrow, anyway. He won't care."

Kailey nodded. "Dad? What time do you have to work tomorrow?"

"Whenever I want to. That's the beauty of being self-employed."

The medic beside him rolled his eyes. Kailey smiled. She liked this paramedic. She sensed a sense of humor in him.

"But I'll probably start at seven like I usually do," Dad said.

"You're so tough, Dad."

"I know." He winked at her.

"Thanks for coming with."

Dad glanced at her. "You're welcome, honey. Any time." He took her mitted hand in his own and squeezed it.

"Will you let me squeeze your hand when they set it?"

"So long as you don't break my hand."

"Deal."

When they got to the hospital, Kailey was wheeled in on her stretcher. It was a long night of waiting and x-rays. Dad kept his word and held her hand while they set her leg. Kailey had to go back a couple days later for them to cast it, since it was too swollen for anything but bandages. They gave her medication for her pain and she fell asleep on the way home.

Kailey was still sleeping when Chelsey left the house as quietly as she could the following morning. The doctor had said Kailey would need to keep the cast on her leg for six weeks, which meant Chelsey needed some other way to get to the top of the hill. That's what she was determined to do. Mom needed to help Kailey at the moment, and Chelsey didn't want to be in the way.

"I can do this," Chelsey muttered to herself as she closed the front door and turned around. This is where she met her first challenge.

The front steps.

"Oh no!" Chelsey cried. "I hate steps. I can't do this. I can't do this." The image of Kailey being lifted out of the house the night before played in Chelsey's head and she took a deep breath. "Kailey does everything for me. I can do this for her."

She gripped the railing with her right hand while still holding onto her bag with her left. "I can do all things through Christ who strengthens me. I can do all things through Christ who strengthens me."

It took a couple minutes to get down those three steps. She was breathing heavily when she finished, but that didn't matter. What did matter was that she *was* finished. With determination, she set her face toward the hill—and Logan's house. A light bulb went off in her head. She smiled and began the next part of her journey.

Her father's instructions about loving Logan, and Kailey's warning to stay away from him, played through her head as she walked up his driveway. *He's mean. Don't do it. He won't help you. Stop it! He will too! Everyone has some good in them, and how am I supposed to show him Jesus if I never talk to him? He doesn't deserve to know Jesus. He won't believe you anyway. He thinks you're a retard. Stop! Stop!* Her mind fought back and forth and her legs kept walking.

She pulled herself up the Stewarts' two front steps and rang the doorbell, holding the button for exactly three seconds. She counted. *Kailey is going to be* so *mad. It doesn't matter. Right now I can run faster than her.*

A head topped with bedhead answered the door.

"I need to speak with Logan, please," she said.

"What? I'm Logan."

"Really?" Chelsey looked him up and down. He was wearing plaid pajama pants; no socks, no shirt. His voice was sounded foggy and his eyes looked even foggier. "Hello, Logan."

"What do you want? And which one are you?" he shook his head and rubbed his right eye.

"I'm Chelsey," she said and smiled, revealing *all* her teeth. "Kailey broke her leg last night after church when she slipped on the kitchen floor that Mom waxed on Saturday. Will you take me to the bus?"

Logan looked around and then shut the door.

"Hey!" Chelsey stood in shock for a moment. *Now what?* She took and deep breath, stood up a little taller and rang the door for exactly three seconds. *Kailey needs this. Kailey needs this.*

Logan answered the door again. "Go away! I'm not helping you!"

"Please!" she begged. "Mom is busy helping Kailey, and I can't get up the hill by myself!"

He rolled his eyes and said a four-letter word and shut the door again.

Chelsey pouted. She picked up her bag and began to leave when she saw his bike in the garage. She smiled a sneaky little smile as she put her bag down and walked toward it.

CHAPTER THIRTEEN

Logan left the house through the garage. The garage smelled like dirt thanks to the bags of potting soil stacked against the east wall. His mother was going to do some transplanting later that week. Her blue Jetta took up half the space in the garage and the shelf with extension cords, pots, and the Christmas tree took up the rest. He walked down the steps and stopped when he saw his neighbour standing on the driveway.

"I'm not helping you," he said, and walked toward his bike. He stopped. Where was his bike? He had left it there that previous night. *Weird.* "Where'd it go?" he muttered, scratching his head and turning around.

"I hid it," Chelsey said, sassy as could be with a triumphant look on her upturned face.

"What?" he whirled around. His heart started to thump wildly. *She hid my bike? She stole it! I need my bike!*

"Now you have to walk with me." She lifted her chin just a little higher and picked up her bag.

The little feeling of anger that had started in Logan's chest grew to wrath. He grabbed Chelsey's shoulders and held them tight. "Tell me where it is!"

"You're hurting me," she whimpered, locking her tear-filled eyes with his sparking blue ones.

"Then you should give me back my bike." He shook her.

"I'll tell you after school, once we're home," she whispered.

Logan shook her again and then let her go. She rubbed her arm where he had held her and a tear trickled down her chin. He spun around and scanned the garage. *Where is it? Where is it?* He growled and pulled the hair on the sides of his head. *Why does this retard need to mess with my life?*

"Give me back my bike!"

"No. Help me to the bus."

He looked around one more time but still didn't see the missing bicycle. He came to stand before her, nose to nose. In a controlled voice, he asked, "If I walk with you, do you promise to give back my bike?" He hated that he had stooped to her little game, but saw no other way around it. If he didn't help her, he might never get his bike back, and the sooner he got it back the better, that way she wouldn't break it—or forget where she put it.

She nodded, fright in her eyes.

"Fine. I'll help you. But this is the one and *only* time, got it?"

She nodded again and tried to lift her backpack. Logan walked past her and headed for the hill. *If she wants to walk with me, she better hurry up.*

"Can you help me with my bag? It's too heavy," she asked in a sweet voice that Logan thought must have belonged to someone else.

"No." He kept walking.

"If you don't help me, we'll get left behind."

"No, *you'll* get left behind."

"And *you* will be in big trouble... And you'll never get your bike back."

Logan stopped and scowled.

She held up the strap of her bag and smiled an I-know-something-you-don't-know kind of smile. "Please."

Logan sighed and walked back to her, picked up the bag, and spun on his heel. He looked back to see Chelsey Martin staring after him with her mouth wide open. "Hurry up!"

His command seemed to jerk her into reality. He didn't bother looking back to see if she needed any more help. *Maybe she'll faint or something and I can leave her here.* The birds sang overhead as they continued their great migration south for the winter. A dog barked as they passed its house. Logan would have thrown a rock at it, but that would have required bending over. About halfway up the hill, he heard a new noise: heavy breathing.

"Can you help me, Logan?"

He twisted around to see Chelsey bent over with one hand on her knee and one on her chest.

"I already have your bag." He cocked his head to the side. "You mean you can't get up the hill by yourself *at all?*"

"No," she panted. "Kailey always helps me."

"Well, I'm not St. Kailey," he yelled over his shoulder. "Retard," he muttered under his breath.

"Just because you call me nasty names, doesn't mean I'm going to stop trying!" she yelled back.

"Stop trying what?" *This is stupid. I'm yelling at this idiot girl who is making us both late for the bus.*

"I'm not going to stop trying to love you!" she screamed, then lost her breath, and gasped for air again.

Logan spun around and marched back down the hill to stand before her. "I don't need *anyone* to love me, especially not you!"

"Yes, you do." She looked up at him and puffed. There was a light in her eye that scared him.

"Why would you want to love me? You like boys who beat you?"

"Not *that* kind of love, silly!" She used the same tone of voice his mother had used when he was little and being disobedient. "I'm trying to love you because Daddy says I have to, because Jesus loves me even though I hurt Him." She looked at him and sighed. "Now will you *please* help me."

"Do it yourself!"

"I can't!" She stomped her foot.

"Well, I don't care if you go to school or not."

"If I don't come because you left me on this here hill, Mrs. Brown will tell Mr. Finley and you will be in *big* trouble." Her eyes flashed. Mr. Finley, the principal, was a stern-looking man who none of the children liked very much because he was always upset about something. Besides that, he didn't have a sense of humor—or if he did, he chose not to entertain it. Logan knew this well. He could see it now: Mrs. Brown telling Mr. Finley and then Mr. Finley calling him into his office and adding to his chore list at school. He and Mr. Finley were well acquainted.

Chelsey walked up to him and took his hand in hers.

"Get away from me!" he bellowed, pushing her away.

Big tears welled up in her eyes. "But..."

"I'm going to leave you here if you don't stop it. Now come on!" Logan ignored her tears and proceeded to march up the hill. Chelsey stumbled behind him with a sob. *Stupid girl! If she didn't want to get hurt, she should have just left my bike alone. Then I could have biked up the hill and she could have stayed home where she belongs.* Logan dropped her bag on the grass at the top of the hill as the bus drove up. He made it up the first two steps when her voice stopped him again.

"I need help."

"What?"

"I can't climb up the steps. I need help."

He rolled his eyes and descended the steps again. He threw her bag into the front seat. She instructed him to climb in backward while she took his hands. It was a painfully slow process for them both. Logan left her in the front seat and went to take his own place at the back of the bus. He scowled to himself as more students got on. He saw some brown-haired chick take her seat beside Chelsey. *Good, she can help that pea brain down. I've had enough of helping others for one week.*

CHAPTER FOURTEEN

Mark Davis stood with his friends and waited for Chelsey to walk by. He hadn't seen Kailey all day. *Where is she?*

"Right, Mark?"

"What?" Mark turned sharply to see Al grinning at him.

"I said, 'Don't worry Dan, that staring off into space look will disappear once he knows what's up with a certain blonde,' right?"

Mark looked at Dan, who also wore a smirk. "Sure, whatever," he said with a shrug.

"I think she might be a redhead actually," Dan said.

Chelsey walked by lugging her book bag.

"See you guys later," Mark said and walked toward her.

Al and Dan watched their smitten friend walk away, then grabbed each other's shoulders and laughed.

Mark ignored them. "Hey Chelsey, how's Kailey doing?"

Chelsey turned around. "Oh, she broke her leg, goodbye Mark," she answered shortly, resuming her walk.

"Bye." Mark scratched his head. *What's wrong with her?*

Amanda helped Chelsey into the bus at the end of the day. Chelsey slid over to make room for her friend in the front seat. The bus jerked to a halt before Baldwin Street. Amanda threw their bags into the grass and helped Chelsey down. Chelsey waited while Amanda pulled on the backpack and swung the knapsack over her shoulder, and then they joined hands and walked down the hill.

"How will you get home?" Chelsey asked.

"I'll just walk. It's not that far."

"Will your mom worry about where you are?"

"No, I'll call her when I get to your house."

"Okay, we have a phone you can use."

Amanda smiled. "Thank you, Chelsey, that's very kind of you."

"What are you going to do for the Christmas program this year?"

"I don't know. It's not for another two months, so I haven't really thought about it. Maybe I'll play my tambourine and dance." Amanda winked at her.

"I don't think you will."

"Why not?"

"I don't think your dad will let you."

"Probably not. What are you going to do?"

"Probably sing while Kailey plays the piano."

"That would be nice. Here we are." Amanda helped Chelsey up the steps of the redbrick house and opened the door. "Honey! I'm home!" she hollered and dropped their bags on the floor before slipping off her sneakers.

"Hello Amanda, how are you?" Mrs. Martin walked into the entranceway wearing an apron with a dishtowel thrown over her shoulder.

"Hello, Mrs. Martin." Amanda smiled. "I'm doing well. I just thought I'd return your daughter to you. Can I use your phone to call my mom and tell her where I am?"

"Of course. You know where it is. Kailey's sleeping on the couch."

"I'll wake her up to say 'hey' once I'm done calling Mom." Amanda slipped past Mrs. Martin and walked down the hallway. She picked up the receiver and was about to dial when she heard Mrs. Martin's voice.

"How did you get up the hill this morning, sweetheart? When I finished with Kailey I was going to drive you up, but you were gone."

Amanda stood in the hallway beside the phone and waited. She had just assumed that Mrs. Martin had taken Chelsey to the bus.

"A friend helped me," Chelsey replied and bit into something.

"Is this friend helping you tomorrow?"

"Yes."

Amanda picked up the phone and called her mother. "Hey, Mom. I walked Chelsey home from school today. I'm just going to say hi to Kailey and then I'll walk home. Love you, too. Bye!" She returned the receiver to its home on the wall and went to the living room. Kailey lay on the couch with an afghan over her and a book on her chest. Her hair was greasy and her face white. Her breathing was even, letting out a small snore every couple breaths. Amanda smiled. She took a pen and quickly wrote a note:

Amanda was here and says "hey, come back to school" love ya ;)

Then she popped into the kitchen to said goodbye to Mrs. Martin, Chelsey, and Devin, let herself out, and walked home.

"Who helped you today?" Dad asked Chelsey at the dinner table. Chelsey sat beside Devin and Kailey sat across from her with her leg up on a chair. Crazy Daisy sat on her mat by the back door, licking her paw with all the sophistication a house cat could muster.

"Amanda helped me, but she couldn't stay for supper."

"But who helped you to the bus?" Kailey asked.

Chelsey put down her glass of water "Pass the garlic bread, please."

Mom passed it.

"Chelsey?"

"Yes, Kailey? Does your foot hurt? Do you need more ice?"

"Who helped you up the hill, Chelsey?"

Chelsey swallowed, looked at her plate, and muttered, "Logan did." She quickly spooned more noodles into her mouth.

"*What?*" Kailey looked up, surprised and cross at the same time.

Chelsey glanced at her as nonchalantly as possibly. "Yes, Logan helped me. I just went over and asked him." She stood and walked to the fridge.

"*You* asked *him?*" Kailey sat up straighter. "Chelsey, I told you to stay away from him!"

"But he was nice," Chelsey lied. Guilt rose her stomach, but she pushed it away. She stuck her head in the fridge and muttered, "After I hid his bike so he had to walk with me."

"Why did you ask him? Chelsey, I thought we talked about this."

Chelsey sighed and looked over her shoulder with her left hand still holding the fridge door open. "Because he's our neighbour and you couldn't help me, and I didn't want to bug Mom because she was helping you."

"How did you get your bag up the hill?"

"Helicopter," Chelsey muttered again.

"What?" Devin's head snapped up.

"He carried it. What do you think?"

"Chelsey, the refrigerator is not a television. Shut the door," Dad said. He looked to his other kids. "What's wrong with Logan helping Chelsey?"

"He's mean," Kailey said.

"He's fine," Chelsey called from the refrigerator.

"Can you please come back to the dinner table now, miss?" Mom asked.

Chelsey grabbed the Parmesan and shut the door harder than she needed to. Crazy Daisy meowed and scampered off. Chelsey stomped back to her chair, sat down, and sprinkled the cheese on top of her macaroni. She frowned, rested her head in her left hand, and spooned the slimy redness into her mouth.

The family sat in silence and watched her. Dad deciphered a storm brewing above her head, complete with black clouds. It was only a matter of time before they witnessed the thunder, lightning, and rain.

Kailey broke the silence. "Chelsey."

"No, Kailey."

"Chelsey."

Chelsey looked up and glared at her sister across the table.

There's the lightning, Dad thought.

"No, Kailey. Stop being such a selfish, judgmental, high and mighty..." words failed Chelsey and she stopped.

"Chelsey!"

"No!" she yelled, rising to stand.

And here comes the thunder.

"Stop now, Kailey. For once in your life let me make my own decisions and leave me alone!" Tears poured down her cheeks. "I'm excused," she sobbed and fled from the table. A few seconds later they all heard her door slam.

CHAPTER FIFTEEN

On Tuesday morning, Logan was still without his bike. He hadn't walked Chelsey home the day before, so she hadn't revealed the secret hiding place and she didn't intend to let it slip now. Mom helped her down their front steps before Kailey woke up.

"Is it really safe for him to help you?" Mom asked.

"Yes," Chelsey said decidedly.

"Then you may go ask him to help you again. If he can't, come back and I'll drive you up. I trust you to make the right decision." Mom's eyes held concern.

"I will. Thanks, Mom." Chelsey gave her mother a hug.

Chelsey walked down the sidewalk to Logan's house with determination. "Mom said she trusted me to make the right decision. Dad said I have to love Logan. I can do this. Right, Jesus? Will you help me?" She slowly climbed up Logan's two front steps and held the doorbell down for exactly three seconds.

"What do you want?" Logan answered the door with a scowl. "No, let me guess, your sister is still stuck with a bad leg."

Chelsey stared up at him. He was only wearing his pajama pants and a head full of wild hair. "Yes," she answered shortly. "She broke her leg Sunday night when we came home from church, so she can't come to school until tomorrow."

"That's why you shouldn't go to church," he mumbled.

"How would you know? Have you ever gone to church?" Chelsey placed her hands on her hips and raised her eyebrows. "You can come to church with us this Sunday if you like!"

"I'd rather not get a broken leg." Logan rolled his eyes and shut the door.

Chelsey pushed the doorbell down.

Logan stuck his head out the door.

Chelsey smiled.

"What?" he growled.

"Will you help me to the bus again?" she asked with the biggest smile she could muster.

"No."

Chelsey stared at the top of Logan's head.

"What are you looking at?" he demanded, touching his forehead self-consciously.

"You sure look funny with your hair like that!" she said, pointed to the top of his head, and giggled.

"Yeah, well, don't tell anyone."

"Let me in."

His eyebrows rose and Chelsey took a step back.

"Please," she added a little shyly.

"Why?" He frowned a deep, scary kind of frown that would have made her cry if she hadn't been so determined.

"Because it's cold out here and I need to wait for you to be ready."

"What?"

"Well you can't go to school looking like that." She pushed past him and stood in the front hallway. The ceiling was high, providing lots of wall space for paintings of wild animals from Africa and the Great White North. She studied the elephant, cheetah, killer whale, wolves, walrus, prairie dogs, and lion. It felt a little imposing with all those great animals staring down at her. Even the prairie dogs, because they reminded her a bit of mice and she wasn't fond of mice at all.

"If I walk with you, will you leave me alone?" Logan asked.

"Maybe," Chelsey whispered as she gazed around her in wonder. "Did you paint these?"

Logan looked around and scratched up his nose. "I think my mom got them from yard sales."

"They're interesting." Chelsey met Logan's eyes. "I'll wait right here while you finish getting ready. We need to leave soon." Logan was about to protest again. "I still have your bike," she said.

"I'll be ready in a minute." Logan went upstairs. *She is such a pain! I'm glad she's not my sister,* he thought to himself as he pulled on dark jeans, a navy polo shirt, and a gray sweater. He buckled his belt and shook his head. *Good thing Mitch isn't here. He'd roast her alive.* He snorted. *Or maybe she'd make sport of him—that'd be great!* He smiled a nasty smile, thinking of the bossy girl downstairs telling his annoying, know-it-all brother to smarten up. *Maybe then he wouldn't come around so much asking Mom for money.*

He walked down the stairs and found Chelsey where he'd left her. He pulled on his shoes. "Okay, let's go," he said, opening the door. They both stepped out and Logan shut the door behind them.

"What about your mom?"

"What about her?"

"Aren't you going to say 'goodbye' to her?"

"Why?"

"Because you're supposed to," she answered matter-of-factly.

"Why's that?" He put his hand on his hip to copy her.

"I don't know, but *I* always do." She rolled her eyes.

Logan sighed, stuck his head in the door, and yelled. "Goodbye, Mom!" He didn't wait for a reply before shutting the door again. He turned back to her.

She nodded her approval. Standing with her nose in the air, she reminded him of the snotty stepsisters in *Cinderella*. He wrinkled his nose at the thought and then picked up both their bags and trudged up the hill, thankful none of his other friends lived on Baldwin Street.

Chelsey survived her computer class in the morning and then walked to the cafeteria.

"Hey, Chelsey."

She turned around to see Mazie walking toward her. Mazie's blond, blue, and pink hair was pulled onto two buns on the top of her head with a significant amount of hair protruding from both. She wore green skinny jeans, a loose pink dress shirt, and a ripped jean jacket.

"Hi Mazie," Chelsey said cheerfully.

"Is it true your sister got hit by a truck?" Mazie asked.

"No, she slipped on the wax floor."

"Oh. Not as exciting, but still pretty cool."

Chelsey shrugged. "I guess. I thought it was still exciting."

"When is she coming back?"

"Tomorrow. The cast is being put on today."

"Cool. English is boring without her." Mazie looked off into the distance for a long moment, then snapped her head back and looked at Chelsey again. "What? Oh. See you around," she said and walked away.

Chelsey blinked four times and continued on her way to the cafeteria.

After school, Uncle Bruno waved her down in the parking lot. Chelsey grinned. He got out of his truck and gave her a huge hug. "Hey there, girl. Would you like a lift home?" he asked with a booming voice.

"Yes!" she yelled right back at him, and climbed up into his truck.

Uncle Bruno put the truck into first gear and off they went. The radio was playing softly until Chelsey recognized a song and turned it *way* up. The two looked at each other and immediately began an off-key duet with Tim McGraw. They had moved on to Rascal Flats and Kenny Chesney when Uncle Bruno saw red and blue lights in his rearview mirror.

"Uh oh," he muttered, pulling over and turning down the radio.

"What is it?"

"The police. I'm even wearing my seatbelt." Uncle Bruno opened the glove box and rummaged around to find his ownership and insurance. A square piece of paper fell out. Chelsey picked it up off the floor as the officer came to the window.

"License please," he said. His thick brown hair stuck out under his hat and his mustache twitched as he read Uncle Bruno's information to himself. Overall he looked like the type of man who ate tomatoes. "Do you know why I pulled you over?"

"No. If I did, I wouldn't have done whatever it was I was doing," said Uncle Bruno.

"Sir, have you been drinking?"

Chelsey giggled.

"No," said Uncle Bruno.

"Sir, you were swerving all over the road. May I ask why?"

Uncle Bruno thought for a moment. "Well, we were just singing along with the radio and I guess I got a little too excited."

The officer frowned.

Chelsey giggled again.

Uncle Bruno turned to her. "You're being no help at all."

"Sorry," she said meekly.

"Do you know this man?" the officer asked Chelsey.

"Yes, he's my uncle."

"Will you please see to it that your uncle refrains from singing along with the radio for the rest of your journey?"

"Yes, sir."

"Good. Have a good day, Bruno—drive safe!" the officer called and walked back to his vehicle.

"What a turkey. Chelsey, can you believe I went to high school with that guy?" Uncle Bruno put the truck in first gear again and they were off. "He pulls me over all the time. Probably seems like a big joke to him. Well, he won't be laughing when I put it on the radio for tomorrow's morning show."

Bruno turned to see Chelsey's reaction, but she wasn't listening. Her head was bent over the picture she held on her lap. "Chelsey?" Uncle Bruno asked quietly.

He heard her sob.

He parked the truck on the side of the road and reached over to give her a hug. "Okay, okay," he whispered and held her close.

"Do you…miss him…too?" Chelsey asked in a broken voice. Then her hiccups started.

"I miss him every day, honey."

"Sometimes…hiccup…I forget…hiccup."

Bruno held her back and looked in her eyes. "Chelsey, it's okay. Life moves on. He would be proud of you if he were here."

"Really?" She wiped her eye.

"I promise." Uncle Bruno wiped the tears under her other eye with his thumb. "You think you're ready to go home now?"

She gave him a small smile and nodded. "Okay."

"Good." He gave her one last squeeze and coaxed the truck back onto the road. Chelsey put the picture back into his glove box and shut it. She sighed and looked out the window. Neither sang on the way home.

CHAPTER SIXTEEN

"How are you going to get up the hill tomorrow?" Devin asked Kailey at the dinner table that evening.

"I don't know, but I can't miss anymore school." She picked up her pork chop with her fingers and bit. Her foot was resting on another chair beside her, where Chelsey normally sat. The doctor had examined her leg that morning and traded the bandages for a blue cast. Chelsey had been the first to sign it.

"I was going to visit Grandma tomorrow and need to leave early," Mom said, looking around the table. Grandma Wilkerson had been steadily getting worse over the last few years. She had fallen the summer before and broken her hip; after that, she had never really regained her health. Grandpa did his best to help her, but every couple weeks Mom would go and sit with her mother so her father could take some time off.

"Don't worry." Chelsey smiled at her mother and thrust more potatoes into her mouth. "I know how she can get up the hill," she said around her mouthful.

"How are *you* going to do *that?*" Devin asked. "You can't even get up the hill by yourself."

"You'll see," Chelsey responded in a sing-song voice.

Kailey wasn't so sure she would like whatever Chelsey had up her sleeve, but she didn't say anything. Chelsey's words the night before about her being judgmental and selfish played through her head again.

After dinner she went to the living room and read a book until Devin and Chelsey were done the dishes, then the three of them watched a movie.

Logan and Nog trotted home after playing catch at the park. Nog's pink tongue hung out of his mouth and swung back and forth like a pendulum as he ran. Logan was deep in thought. *I don't understand why she keeps coming over and asking for help. I have* never *been nice to her and I never will be.*

She said she wants to love you.

Which is the stupidest thing ever.

She said it's the right thing to do.

People don't do stuff because it's the right thing to do. People do stuff because they want something. What does she want from me? She knows I will never be her friend, that she doesn't belong with me and my friends, that she's a total loser. Tomorrow if she comes I'll shut the door in her face and leave her there.

Then she'll just keep ringing your doorbell and Mom will want to know what's going on.

Yeah well, then Mom can answer the door.

She'll make you help the dumb chick. And you'll never get your bike back.

Logan's face clouded. He had searched for his bike to no avail. He thought about calling the police, but he didn't want them in his life any more than they already were. The old man hadn't reported anything from the convenient store, much to his relief. He and Nog jogged up to their house. Logan opened the gate to the backyard and let Nog off the leash. He stretched and watched the dog chase his tail, then he went inside to see if Mom had bought anymore milk and popcorn. *You'll never get your bike back.* He shook his head, filled a glass of milk and put the bag back in the fridge, then went to sit before the TV, pushing the thoughts of Chelsey Martin out of his head.

"You stay here and I'll go get the wagon." Chelsey left her sister sitting in the front entranceway and walked out the door. Mom had left earlier to go stay with Grandpa and Grandma, Dad was at work, and Devin had stayed overnight at his friend's house after dinner the night before so they could work on a school project.

It took Chelsey a several minutes to get down their steps, but she felt very accomplished to be able to do it by herself. Logan's front steps didn't have a handrail, so it took her longer to get up them. When she finally made it, a smile of satisfaction lit up her face. She held the doorbell down, *one, two, three.*

Logan opened the door. Chelsey had expected the usual pajama pants and bedhead, but the Logan before her wore jeans, a sweater, and socks. His hair was even combed…sort of. At least he had it gelled and stuck up straight in the front; this worked for him, though Chelsey supposed not everyone would look good with their hair sticking out in every direction. His school bag sat by the door waiting for him, or perhaps for her.

"Wow, what happened to the crazy hair and PJ pants?" she asked.

"I figured you'd come over wanting help, so I was ready," he answered in a dry voice that sounded like he didn't want to seem too concerned whether she came or not.

"Oh." She sighed and looked up at him. "Well, all I need is your wagon. I saw it in your garage last time I was in there."

"Oh. Bring it back when you're done." He sent her a skeptical glance and then shut the door in her face.

Logan looked out the window as she walked to his garage. He shrugged. "If she needed my help, she *would* ask." He went to the kitchen to get his waffle out of the toaster. His mom was sitting by the island drinking tea and reading the paper in her robe and slippers. Her brown-gray hair had yet to be tamed after its adventure with the curlers the night before.

"Was that the girl?" she asked. "Did she need your help again?"

"Nope, just the wagon." Logan turned to see her smiling at him over her mug. "What?"

"What did she need it for?"

"I don't know."

The doorbell rang.

"I think you're about to find out." His mom went back to her paper.

Logan stuffed the waffle in his mouth and went to answer the door again.

"What?"

Chelsey looked up at him. "I need your help."

He opened the door wider and waved her inside while he swallowed his breakfast. "With what?" he asked while he pulled his shoes on. He noticed she didn't have her school bag.

"Is your mom here?" Chelsey changed the subject so quickly that Logan had to think for a second before answering.

"Yes."

"My mom left before I got up. She went to visit Grandma and I didn't get to say goodbye to her. Do you think it would be okay if I said goodbye to your mom instead? Please?" Her entire face pleaded with him.

Logan shrugged and rolled his eyes. "Fine with me." He tied his shoe and stood up. "Well?"

"You say it first," she whispered loudly.

He sighed again. "Goodbye, Mom!"

"Goodbye, Logan's mom!" Chelsey yelled immediately after him and then went out the door.

As Logan closed the door, they both heard, "Goodbye, Logan's friend!"

Chelsey grinned at him.

He ignored it. "Where's your bag? What do you need help with?"

"Kailey can't get into the wagon by herself. That's all I need your help for." Chelsey led the way back to her house. As she slowly ascended the front steps, Logan wondered how awkward this was going to be. He considered running away but the memory of his bike kept him where he was.

CHAPTER SEVENTEEN

Kailey sighed in relief when she saw Chelsey's head peek inside the front door. "*Thank you* for not getting Logan. I don't need help." She sent her sister a delighted grin, which quickly faded when she saw a dark mass of hair. "Oh no!" she wailed and leaned back in her chair.

"Don't be afraid," Chelsey comforted her, coming to her chair and taking her arm. "He's here to help us."

"Chelsey, I am so mad at you. I think if I didn't have a bad leg I would throw you in the shower and turn it on real cold!" Kailey hissed at her twin, knowing Chelsey hated cold water almost as much as she hated climbing stairs.

Logan stepped in the door, looking ill at ease. "I can go," he told Chelsey.

"No, we need you." Chelsey grabbed his arm to stop him.

Kailey sent her sister one last glare before turning her fiery green eyes to Logan. "I just need help down the steps," she said coolly.

"Okay," he said tentatively. *How are we going to get her down the steps? Man, this is awkward. Lori would be so ticked off if she saw me right now. I wish I had never gotten out of bed this morning. What would they do on TV?* Suddenly, an idea came to him. "How about if Chelsey takes the crutches and I help Kailey?"

Without a word, Chelsey picked up the crutches and fled out the door. Logan heard her take a deep breath when she reached the first step.

He turned to Kailey. She looked like she would rather die than let him touch her. "Here we go," he muttered and took a step toward her.

"I need my jacket," Kailey said.

She's angry. "Where is it?" *This is stupid. Stupid.*

She nodded toward the coat rack. "It's the dark blue jean one," she said.

He took it off its hook and handed it to her. It took her a minute to put it on, but once she was ready she looked up at him expectantly, like she was waiting for a miracle.

Well, she sure isn't going to get one today, Logan thought, but replied out loud with a bit more grace. "Ready?"

Her eyes flashed. "Yes."

They're both snobby, Logan thought as he came to stand beside her. "Okay." He stood on her right side, the side with the broken leg, and put his arm under her arms. "Put your left leg down and we'll lift on three." Kailey did as he instructed. "One, two, *three,*" he grunted the last number and heaved her up. Kailey put her weight on her good foot to keep from falling. She wobbled for a second but Logan supported her as a crutch and she stood with a look of determination on her face.

She's heavier than I thought she would be. Logan didn't utter a word. He pushed open the front door with his free hand. Kailey kept her right arm around Logan's back and shoulders and her left hand touched the garage wall while they made their decent. Logan slipped on the middle step. Kailey let out a little scream and tightened her told on him. He grasped the railing tightly and lifted Kailey a bit to keep her from falling. "You okay?" he asked with an out-of-practice smile.

She blew a lock of hair out of her eyes and leveled him with a look. "Sure, but let's try not to do that again," she answered coolly.

Logan frowned.

"Come on!" Chelsey yelled. Logan started to move again and Kailey had no choice but to follow his lead.

Getting her into the wagon proved to be a bit more difficult. Logan instructed Chelsey to keep Kailey's leg off the ground while he helped her in. Once she was seated, Logan looked from one girl to the other. "Well, my work here is done," he announced, dusted off his hands, and strolled away.

Chelsey smiled down at Kailey. "You look like Cinderella off to the ball."

"Go get our backpacks," Kailey grunted. Her leg throbbed. *This could very well be the worst day of my life. How embarrassing! The biggest bully in school helping me down our front steps. Not cool. Not cool.*

Chelsey came back with one bag at a time.

Kailey looked from the bags sitting on the sidewalk to her sister. "How are you going to get me and the bags up the hill by yourself?" she asked. *Wonder what Miss planned-it-perfect will say to that.*

"Logan!" Chelsey yelled.

"No, no, no," Kailey groaned. *Please tell me you aren't going to get him to help us again! Please no!*

Logan turned around and looked at them from his place on the sidewalk. He'd gone a fair distance in his hurry to escape.

"Chelsey!" Kailey cried. *Why can't she just keep her mouth shut for once in her life?*

"We need your help!" Chelsey screeched in a voice that went a few octaves too high for anyone's ears. Logan trotted toward them.

He stood in front of the wagon and looked down at the two blondes before him. "Do you think we could put the bags on your lap?" he asked Kailey, his left eyebrow raised slightly. This was going to be a challenge. Something inside reminded him he liked challenges now and again.

"Sure," she answered. "Do you think you call pull me and all the bags up the hill?"

He heard the sarcasm in her voice and glared at her. "Not if I don't want to. But then you'll be stuck in this wagon in front of your house till your mom comes home."

"I can push!" Chelsey offered excitedly.

Logan threw the bags and crutches onto Kailey's lap. She grunted under the weight, but didn't say anything. Logan picked up the handle and began to pull. "We'll stop at my house for my bag," he called back to Chelsey. She didn't hear him. "Okay, stop now." He let go of the handle but Chelsey didn't hear and kept pushing. The wagon smashed into the back of his heel. "Stop, Chelsey!" his heel began to pound.

She obliged. "What?"

"I have to get my bag, so stop pushing, you hurt me!" Logan yelled, his anger exploding as he glowered at her.

A tear came to the corner of her eye, but he ignored it and went to get his bag.

"She didn't hear you," Kailey scolded him. "So don't yell at my sister. She didn't mean to hurt you!"

Logan stared at her. *I wonder if she could make this any more unpleasant than it already is.* "Yes, your royal highness," he said with a scowl, threw his bag carelessly on her lap, picked up the wagon handle, and yelled to Chelsey, "Push!"

CHAPTER EIGHTEEN

The hill proved to be almost too much for them. The wind picked up as they reached the top of the hill, and Logan wondered if it was some sad twist of fate or if Chelsey's God was testing his patience. None of their neighbours had ventured outside; the clouds threatened rain and the sun hid behind them, afraid of getting wet.

Logan pulled with all his might and Chelsey more or less held on instead of pushing like she was supposed to. Kailey had the honour of making sure nothing tumbled down the hill. Her leg was throbbing tremendously by the time they reached the top of the hill. *Lord, I know in your infinite wisdom you decided not to give me a normal sister—but could you at least make the sister I have less embarrassing?*

The stop sign at the top of Baldwin St. came into view. The bright yellow bus turned the corner from Mariana onto Coalgate just as they reached the top of the hill. Logan pulled the wagon to a squeaky halt, Chelsey stood still, breathing heavily, and Kailey pushed everything that had been on her lap off onto the ground. "I hate this hill and this wagon," she moaned.

Kailey's frown met Logan's raised eyebrows as he retrieved his bag from the dirt. He didn't utter a word as he walked away to get on the bus. Chelsey pulled on her knapsack and followed Logan. Kailey sighed again and tried to push herself out of the wagon. A moment of panic came over her as she fell back where she had been sitting.

I can't get up.

"Hey, guys?"

Logan turned.

Kailey swallowed hard. "Could...could you help me get up?"

He dropped his bag and walked toward her. His face maintained its hard lines as he put his arm around her and jerked her up.

Getting into the bus proved to be a great challenge. They couldn't fit side by side to climb up the steps, so Logan stood behind her to keep her from falling as she pulled herself up. *They should make people do this on one of those survivor shows,* Kailey thought. *Good thing we always sit in the front.*

Logan plopped her down in the front seat and went back for her sister and their bags. Chelsey was beaming as she took her place and Kailey rolled her eyes. *At least one person is happy with this whole experience.*

Logan dropped their bags at their feet without so much as a glance their way and stalked to the back.

"Well, look who finally made it up the hill so she could go to school!" Amanda grinned at the twins as she took her seat behind them. "I thought you had just up and quit the social scheme."

"That might have been a better alternative," Kailey said.

"Why? You look great. But you always look great. And a certain someone would be *very* disappointed if you became a hermit."

"Who?" Kailey wrinkled her nose.

"Guess."

Mark. "He asked about me?"

Amanda nodded with laughter in her eyes.

"Guess how Kailey got up the hill," Chelsey said. "She sat in the wagon and Logan and I pulled her up," Chelsey explained loud enough for the entire bus to hear. Kailey poked her.

Amanda looked from one twin to the other. "Really?"

"Do you think we *could* make up a story like that?" Kailey asked.

"Well, you have been sitting around taking pain meds for the last couple days."

"Amanda!"

"Hey! It's true! But I believe you."

"This is so embarrassing." Kailey covered her head with her hands and sunk a little lower into her seat.

"Oh, you'll survive. I'll help you off the bus when we get to school." Amanda patted her friend on the back.

"Thank you, Amanda. Did you hear that, Chelsey? Amanda's going to help us off the bus." Kailey glanced at her sister, who remained silent; she was too enamored in a conversation with Mrs. Brown, the bus driver, about someone named Roger.

Logan marched past the twins and stepped off the bus. They didn't need his help anyway—their friend was helping them. He joined his friends at the bike racks and looped his arm around Lori and gave her a kiss. She kissed him back.

"Hey," she whispered against his ear and then leaned into him again.

"Hey guys, it's the look-a-like retards." Bret Wilson's voice made them look up.

Kailey walked between Amanda and Chelsey. Chelsey was struggling with her book bag and Amanda carried her bag as well as Kailey's.

"Which one is the one with the bum leg? The retard or her stupid sister? Maybe now we'll finally be able to tell them apart." The other's joined in his laugher, except Logan. He was thinking. How did he tell them apart? When they talked it was easy, because Kailey was usually mad at him, but when it came to just looking at them it was more difficult.

"I heard she broke it when her idiot sister pushed her in front of a bus."

"Wow, close family," Bret muttered. "Did she do it on purpose? Doesn't she know buses can do some serious damage? Though, I guess they're close to the same size."

Logan looked up just in time to catch Chelsey's eyes; they were filled with hurt like the lost baby seal he'd seen on a documentary the night before. She blinked slowly and he saw one lone tear slide down her cheek.

Just one.

A bad feeling rose from the pit of his stomach and came up to his mouth. He swallowed hard and looked away. He kissed Lori one more time. "Got to get to class," he muttered, and walked away.

"Okay, did you really just slip on the floor? Because *everyone* is saying you got hit by a bus," Mazie asked after Kailey hobbled down the row of desks in English class.

"Yes, I slipped on the floor on Sunday night and landed wrong." Kailey awkwardly took her seat, leaning her crutches against her desk.

"Not as exciting, but still cool that your leg is blue. Your hair looks fantastic." Mazie smacked her gum.

Kailey turned and looked at her with a quizzical expression. "What?"

"Yeah, your hair looks great."

"I meant about getting hit by a bus. Everyone thinks that?"

"Oh, yeah, I heard you got hit by a bus and then I was going to ask if you looked so nice today because you're going to the courthouse to sue the driver—but since you slipped on the floor I guess it's your own dumb fault and you have no one to sue."

Kailey shook her head and looked down at her desk. *Good thing I left my books here. I don't know how I would manage with books and crutches.*

"How you going to carry your stuff?" Mazie asked, echoing Kailey's thoughts. "Maybe you could carry it on your head like those migrant workers from Mexico that my uncle hires every year. But I bet your balance is off because of your crutches. So maybe you should just plead 'no homework' for the next bit till you can actually walk."

"Thanks, Mazie, you're a true friend." Kailey reached down to get the pen she'd dropped on the floor when Logan walked in and sat behind her. She shivered.

Mazie leaned over and whispered, "Did you see that? He's not late today!"

That fact had escaped Kailey's notice, but now it struck her that she had never seen him on time before for anything, ever. She found her pen and was about to reply when Mr. Marksdale entered.

"Good morning, class!" he greeted with a bright smile.

Morning people should all be shipped to an island together and not allowed to leave till they learn to be quieter, Kailey thought.

"Is everyone ready to dive into another exciting class of English?" He stood in front of his desk and scanned the room, then he stretched to his tiptoes. "Is that Mr. Stewart sitting behind Miss Martin?" He called all his students either Mr. or Miss. Kailey thought it had to do with some kind of psychology, the I-respect-you-so-you-should-respect-me idea. For the most part this seemed to work for him. Assignments were handed in on time and students didn't goof off in his class as much as in other classes.

Mr. Marksdale walked down the aisle. "Glad to see you're up and about again, Ms. Martin. Your sister said you broke your beak on Sunday night; we're glad you're well enough to be with us." Kailey returned his smile. "And Mr. Stewart, how nice of you to join our class on time. Your presence is greatly appreciated."

Mr. Marksdale went back to stand behind his desk. "Over the next few weeks, we're going to studying Shakespeare. Please open your copy of *The Taming of the Shrew*."

CHAPTER NINETEEN

It was slow going down the school hallway. *Stupid crutches,* Kailey thought. *I feel like I can't do anything with these things. I can't even open the door for myself. And I am* so *slow.* She growled under her breath as her crutches squeaked, announcing to everyone her arrival. Heads turned to watch her go.

"Kailey!"

She turned to see Mark hurrying down the hall toward her. A small smile crept up on her face while she waited. He was wearing a bright red sweater and dark jeans. His blond hair was getting a little long, but she supposed his uncle probably didn't bother to tell him to go get it cut. *Guys do tend to be clueless about stuff like that. But in this case I think it's okay; he looks kinda cute with hair in his eyes. Actually, he always looks cute.*

"Hey," he greeted a little breathlessly, stopping beside her.

"Hey, what's up?"

"I was just wondering if you were okay. I heard you got hit by a bus."

"Why does everyone think I got hit by a bus?" She looked up at Mark. "Sorry, you're the fourth person to ask that and it's getting a little old. I actually slipped on my mom's waxed floor."

Mark's body visibly relaxed in relief. "Oh, good. It would be really bad to be hit by a bus."

"Maybe I should put an article in the school paper so people know what really happened."

"Hey, that's not a bad idea." Mark winked at her.

Was that a for-real wink or an I-feel-awkward-so-I'll-wink kind of wink? "I was just going to my locker, actually."

"Oh, I'll walk with you that far," Mark offered.

"K." Kailey glanced his way and then started her slow journey down the hallway again. "How is it living with your uncle?"

"Oh, fine. He doesn't make cookies like my mom does, but that's okay. I guess beggars can't be choosers."

"You're a beggar?" Kailey's voice held laughter.

"Okay, not really. My parents asked me if I would want to live with Uncle Melvin for the school year this year and I figured, why not? We've always gotten along. Here's your locker. Have a good day, Kailey. Stay away from buses and waxed floors."

"I sure will. See you, Mark." Kailey pivoted on her good foot to face her locker. She worked on the lock for a minute, balancing her crutches against her body with her casted foot up in the air. "Got it," she whispered, and pulled the door open.

"Hey Kailey, how's it going?"

She glanced up to see Al Fisher. "Hey, I just need to get some books for Biology."

"Here, you want me to help you carry them? I'm going past Bio on my way to Chemistry."

"Seriously? That would be fantastic. I was wondering how I would manage. Mark was here talking to me, but then he up and left before he could give me a hand." Kailey piled three books into Al's arms and then shut the locker door and twisted the combination.

"So, what do you think of Mark?" Al asked as they went down the hallway.

Kailey sent him a sidelong glance. "I think he is a fine upstanding young man. What do you think of him?"

"He's my friend, so I get along with him."

"Well, that's good. Why do you ask?"

"Oh, just wondering." They reached the Biology classroom and Al put her books on the table where Maria was sitting.

She sent him a friendly wave. "Thanks Al, I'll talk to you later."

"See you, have fun."

"Oh, we will. We're dissecting frogs today."

Al stuck out his tongue and made a gagging noise as he walked out of the room.

The bus pulled up to the top of Baldwin Street. It groaned and lurched to a stop. Chelsey turned in her seat and watched as Logan plowed his way to the front of the bus. She stuck her arm out to stop him. "Would you help us down? Please?" she asked sweetly.

He glared at her. She met his darkened eyes with an open and hopeful expression in her clear blue eyes, fully believing he would help them. Without a word, he reached across Kailey and picked up their bags. He walked to the top of the steps and was about to throw them out.

"Stop!" Chelsey cried. "Don't do that!"

He sent her a sidelong glance; then, with a great deal of exaggeration, he placed them *gently* outside. He helped Kailey out first, while Chelsey talked to Mrs. Brown.

"Yes," she said. "He doesn't know *anything* about helping so I have to tell him."

"Oh, how very good of you," Mrs. Brown said.

He grunted, pulled on Chelsey's arm, and helped her down the steps, but not before he caught a smile from Mrs. Brown.

"Thank you, Logan, and good luck," she said.

"Thanks," he muttered. The door slammed shut and the bus pulled away. He picked up his bag and started down the hill.

"*Logan!*"

"What, Chelsey?" he called over his shoulder without looking back.

"*Help us!*" she screamed.

He turned around. "You can get her down the hill by yourself!"

"No, I can't get her into the wagon!" Chelsey complained, pointing an accusing finger at Kailey.

Kailey stood close by, leaning on her crutches and being fought over. She might have thought it was funny how her sister bossed one of the biggest bullies in school around—if the circumstances were such that she didn't feel like a piece of meat on a chopping block.

"Please just help us, Logan." Kailey was tired and ready to go home and crash. Truthfully, she was sick of needing other people to help her and it had only been three days. *I just wanted life back to the way it was. Having people help all the time goes against my nature.*

Logan stomped back, obviously ticked off. In fact, he was quite possibly the most ticked off person Kailey had ever seen in real life. He took her crutches from her, laid them on the ground, and then roughly helped her into the wagon, muttering under his breath with the occasional four-letter word mixed in. Once she was seated, he glared down at her and walked away.

Kailey watched Logan's back sway back and forth as he walked down the hill. She turned to her sister. "How are you going to get us down the hill? You have me, yourself, and all our bags. You can't even climb up by yourself."

Chelsey looked confident—too confident. "Don't worry, I can climb up our front steps by myself now."

Kailey rolled her eyes. "So can most two-year-olds."

Chelsey's face fell. "Oh."

"Chelsey, sometimes you have really good ideas. But this isn't one of those times." Kailey tried to keep her voice gentle and kind. She felt her patience wearing thin. *Kind words. Kind words.*

Chelsey stuck her chin up. "I can do it," she said and picked up the handle.

It started out alright. The top of the hill plateaued where the bus picked them up, and it was easy to pull the wagon on that part of the pavement. As soon as the wheels met the incline of the hill, Kailey knew they were going to be in trouble. Chelsey's walk quickly turned into jogging and then into running in order to keep from getting run over by the cart. It jostled and bumped wildly as if driven by frightened horses that had just finished energy drinks. Kailey shrieked and tried to hold onto their bags without being thrown from the wagon. She took a deep breath and screamed, hoping she wasn't taking one step farther from her normal life than those she had already taken.

"Logan!"

CHAPTER TWENTY

Logan turned when he heard Kailey's scream. Her eyes were closed and she was holding onto the wagon's sides with all her might. Chelsey was pulling her down the hill at a rapid speed, moving far more quickly than he had ever seen her move before.

If there had been time, he had no doubt that an angel would have appeared on his right shoulder and a devil on his left. However, he didn't have time to argue with himself; Kailey had already lost one bag and the other was bound to be gone soon, given its current perilous position on her lap. He dropped his bag on the sidewalk, blocking their way, and ran up to get the handle from Chelsey.

"Let go, Chelsey!" he yelled at her as he reached for the handle. She let go and more or less crumpled into the lawn on her left. Logan managed to grasp the handle and bring the wagon to a stop just before his bag.

He looked back at Kailey. Her eyes were still closed tightly and her knuckles were turning white where they gripped the rails. He smiled. She reminded him of Lori's sister, who was afraid of monsters under her bed. He pushed his bag up to the tires to keep the wagon from rolling down the hill and leaned down so that his face met hers. "You can open your eyes now."

She opened one eye, focused on him, then opened her other eye and looked around. "Thank you," she whispered in a small voice. His face was inches from hers. Her head swung back and their eyes met. They stared at each other for a moment and then she blinked.

He stood up and looked for Chelsey. She was making her way down the hill at a much slower pace than before, lugging the bag they had lost in their escapade.

"Oh boy, we were almost flying!" she yelled, waving her arms in excitement.

"It was *not* fun!"

Logan looked down at Kailey. She seemed to be the kind of person who was against having fun. He almost felt sorry for Chelsey, who obviously liked to have fun a great deal. He waited till Chelsey caught up with them and then threw his bag onto the other bags already haphazardly positioned on Kailey's lap, and then began pulling the wagon down the hill again. He tried not to think what Lori would think of him pulling Kailey Martin down their hill and talking to her mentally handicapped sister. He shook his head; hopefully she would never know.

He helped Chelsey back up their front steps and then went back to get Kailey out of the wagon. They were quiet through the ordeal, but when Kailey reached for the doorknob, she took a deep breath and said, "Logan, thank you for helping us up and down the hill today."

"Oh."

"But I still don't trust you, and I want you to stay away from my sister except when it's completely necessary."

"Don't worry. There is no reason in this world that I would *ever* want to spend more time with you or your sister than necessary."

"Good."

"Just don't forget who is helping whom up the hill," he said shortly and walked away. *Why would I ever want to spend more time with those two than I had to? I only helped them because Chelsey still has my bike. What a dumb girl. She is the opposite of popular. She could never be my friend even she wanted to be. Who does she think she is?*

He leaped up his front steps, jerked open the front door, and slammed it soundly behind him. His mother was standing next to the shelf in the living room holding a rag in one hand and a knickknack in the other. She jumped when she heard him come in.

"Logan! Be kind to our front door."

"Mom, that girl is an idiot!"

"Who? Why?" His mother looked confused.

"She told me to stay away from her sister because she doesn't trust me. Like, how stupid! I would never want to be her friend anyway."

"Whose friend?"

"The neighbour girls'. I had to help them down the hill together because the mental one decided she could pull the wagon by herself, which she totally couldn't, and she almost killed her sister so I pulled them down. They're both idiots. Their only friends are their church group people and I definitely don't want to be in that group. Geeks, weirdos…"

"Then why are you so upset?" Mom put the dolphin figurine down and picked up a picture of Logan and Mitch playing at the beach when they were small. Logan had his finger in his ear, trying to remove some sand, and Mitch was grinning from ear to ear with a blue bucket and shovel in his hands.

"Because she had the nerve to think that I would talk to her sister. No one talks to her sister. She's a retard, Mom. No one wants to hang out with retards. I have my own friends."

"I thought you said she said she didn't trust you around her sister."

Logan sat on stairs and looked his mother. His entire face glowered. "Whatever that means. I'm trustworthy. Who's the guy helping them to the bus every morning?"

His mother turned from her dusting. "Trust is earned, Logan."

He held her eyes. She must have seen what she was looking for, because she nodded and went back to her dusting.

He stood and ran up the stairs to his room. *Stupid girls.*

Kailey sat at the piano with her right leg propped up on the chair beside her. The living room was dark. Everyone else was sitting in the kitchen playing cards. Uncle Bruno had come over after helping Aunt Louise get to bed. "She's always sick and no fun at all," he explained when he called earlier to ask if anyone felt like playing with "the old, bored man." It wasn't hard to find someone who wanted to play with Uncle Bruno. He was a horrible cheater and wonderful loser, and generally threw more candy and popcorn than he ate.

Kailey's fingers moved from white to black keys and back again. She didn't know the song she was playing; it came from inside and somehow in the dark it expressed itself more easily. The piano was that friend who let her get everything out. It didn't return her statements with judgment or ask her what she was thinking. Pianos just know things. They patiently let themselves be used for the betterment of others, and they love it. After all, what kind of piano doesn't love to be played? A minor song resounded through the living room, bouncing off the bookshelf and quiet clock.

Chelsey screamed in the kitchen and Devin yelled. There was thumping followed by Uncle Bruno's booming voice. *He must have gotten caught cheating again, and now they're trying to make him pay for it.*

Kailey blocked out the noise and continued to play. It had been an interesting, humiliating, kind of day. And tomorrow would be today's twin. Both looking alike in the interesting—and humiliating—factors. Why Logan had to be the one to help them up the hill and pull her in that ridiculous wagon, she didn't know. She stopped her playing to try to scratch an itch under her cast. She couldn't reach it. She tried to rub the top of her cast to get it and finally gave up. Her fingers went back to their home on the piano and began another song.

She hoped Aunt Louise would be feeling better soon. Uncle Bruno looked sad, and he wasn't even the one who was throwing up all the time. The yelling and screaming in the kitchen had turned into laughter and the smell of popcorn was beginning to drift her way. She finished her song with a chord, and hobbled to the kitchen.

Uncle Bruno left shortly after, giving them all hugs, and then Dad declared the entire household was going to bed.

CHAPTER TWENTY-ONE

Chelsey walked down the aisle Sunday morning and took her seat in the middle of the pew. Devin joined her shortly after, wearing blue dress pants, a white shirt, and a blue bowtie. Kailey had informed him that morning that bowties were out of style, but he said they were coming back in and wore it anyway. Chelsey didn't mind. She thought Devin always looked reasonably nice.

Mrs. Bloomberg was playing the organ slowly. She always played slowly. Chelsey glanced at the bulletin to see who was on to play piano with her. Millie Grimshaw. She groaned. Millie played even more slowly than Mrs. Bloomberg. This was going to be painful.

She glanced across the church and saw Marie walk in with her brother, Rob, behind her. Chelsey's face lit up. She waved. Maria was watching where her feet were going, but Rob caught Chelsey's greeting and waved back. Chelsey poked Devin and pointed to where the Berrys were sitting. Devin smiled and returned Rob's wave.

"If I had a brother, I would want it to be Rob," Chelsey whispered.

"Hey!" Devin looked offended.

"I mean an older brother," Chelsey clarified.

"Good." Devin went back to reading his bulletin.

The Martins invited two elderly couples and three widows over for lunch. After casserole and apple crisp, the family and their guests retired to the living room for tea.

Later, after the second service, Amanda and Maria joined the Martin family for supper.

"I think he really likes you," Amanda said. She sat on the floor of Kailey's bedroom with her back against the wall. Kailey was sitting on the chair before the vanity and Maria was lying on the ground trying to get her back to crack back into place.

"Whatever," Kailey said.

"No, really, Mark looks at you *all the time* and he asked about you when you were gone. If you were in any of the same classes, he would sit beside you and ask you what homework you had."

"I think he's just friendly."

"Well, do you want him to just be friendly? Or would you be okay with it if he really liked you?" Maria asked.

Kailey was quiet for a moment. "I think I'm okay either way," she said slowly.

"Whatever." Amanda rolled her eyes.

"No, really. I'm only fifteen, guys. I can't date for a couple years anyway. And I don't know him very well."

"All good points." Maria sat up and leaned against the bottom bunk. "Besides, boys are weird. I think you should stay away from them."

"How would you know?" Amanda asked.

"I have brothers."

"Which are all amazing," Amanda said.

"They're pretty good brothers, but they're still guys. Guys are weird. They smell weird, they laugh about dumb things, they like to play hockey—"

"They'd probably say the same about us."

"No, they like the way girls smell."

"You guys have talked about this?" Kailey asked.

"Well yeah, I mean, we talk about lots of stuff. One time I came downstairs after taking a shower and Colin said that shampoo is the best smell a girl can smell like. It must be true, because Rob and Terrence agreed."

"Shampoo?" Amanda stared at her.

"Hey, don't judge me. That's what they said."

"There are so many better smells than shampoo," Amanda said. "For example, cinnamon buns."

"How many girls do you know that go around smelling like cinnamon buns?" Kailey asked.

"Maybe they should make a shampoo that smells like cinnamon buns," Maria said.

The girls looked at to the doorway where they heard someone clear their throat.

Devin stood very still with his hand positioned to knock on the open door. "Maria's mom is here to take the girls home," he said.

"How long have you been there, Dev?" Kailey asked.

"All I heard was something about shampoo that smells like cinnamon."

"Sure." Amanda rolled her eyes and stood. "Come on, Maria, we better not keep your mom waiting. Thanks for having us, Kailey. See you at school tomorrow." She rubbed Devin's head on her way out the door.

"Bye Kailey, see you tomorrow! Hope your trip up the hill is uneventful."

"Thanks, Maria. I hope so too. See you guys later!" Kailey walked them to the entranceway and then waved from the front window. Devin stood beside her. "Is that really all you heard, Devin?"

"Yeah, and I think it's dumb. Why wouldn't you make shampoo that smells like pork chops or wings if you want to attract men?" Before Kailey could push him, Devin had run into the kitchen sporting a ridiculous smile.

It became routine for Logan to help the twins up and down the hill every day. After two weeks, he even got up early enough to get dressed and eat breakfast before he heard the doorbell ring for exactly three seconds. He knew his mother watched the episode play out every morning with smug satisfaction, but he chose to ignore it. He wasn't becoming friends with these girls. He was just helping them for the sake of his bike. Once Kailey's leg was healed and they could walk alone again, he would get his bike back and be rid of them.

The end of October was cool and crisp. Logan pulled on his sweater and threw the last bite of his peanut butter toast to Nog before answering the door. Chelsey stood outside with a blue hat perched on her head and her hot pink coat zipped up to her chin.

"Good morning!" she greeted him with bright eyes.

"Hey," he muttered, and let her in while he put on his shoes and found his coat. Chelsey quietly petted Nog while she waited. Logan pushed the dog out of the way and walked to the door. "Bye Mom!" he called.

"Bye, Logan's mom!" Chelsey yelled. Logan shut the door behind them.

Chelsey waited by Logan's house while he went to get Kailey. She tended to be more of hindrance in the whole process than a help. Kailey had managed to get down the steps by the time Logan reached her. He helped her into the wagon, positioned their bags on top of her, shouldered Chelsey's backpack, and pulled her back up the sidewalk toward Chelsey.

The whole ordeal was getting down to a science. Kailey had found she could slide her crutches between her hip and the wagon's side and hold onto the two knapsacks, but adding Chelsey's backpack had proved to be too much and she kept dropping something, causing Logan to stop and go back for it, making the entire trip take longer. When Chelsey's backpack fell for the third time a few days earlier, Logan finally just put it on and everything had gone better.

"Kailey went to the doctor after school yesterday," Chelsey announced when they met up in front of Logan's house.

"Oh," Logan said.

"He said she'll need to keep her cast on for the rest of school, so you will still need to help us."

Logan's entire face frowned at her.

"Okay, he actually said it could come off before Christmas." She smiled at him and tripped. Logan grabbed her arm to steady her. "Oh, thanks."

He grunted.

"Why are you always so grumpy? Don't you like us?"

"Not really."

"Why not?"

"Because girls are weird."

"But you have a girlfriend."

"So?"

"Do you like her?"

"I guess."

"Well, isn't she weird?"

"They're weirder in a group."

Chelsey sighed heavily and trudged ahead. "What's your girlfriend's name?"

"Lori."

"Why is she your girlfriend?"

"Chelsey, maybe Logan doesn't want to talk about it. Maybe you should ask him what he likes to talk about," Kailey said from the wagon.

"Why?" Chelsey called back.

"Because..." Kailey stopped.

Because that's what friends do, Logan thought.

"Fine, what do you like, Logan?"

Silence hung in the air. It was crisp, still air. A flock of Canadian Geese flew overhead on their way south for the winter. A blue jay shared his unpleasant song from the neighbour's tree, and Logan thought he smelled a fresh apple crisp.

"I like math," he said.

"Wow," Chelsey said dryly.

"What?" Logan questioned with a raised eyebrow.

"Okay, math is probably *the* most boring subject on the face of this entire earth. Have you *seen* people who do math all the time? They wear big glasses and sweater vests and their friends probably all smell like calculators—whatever calculators smell like." Chelsey held her mitted hands up to her eyes to illustrate how big their glasses were.

"Yeah right," Logan said.

"What do you think, Kailey?"

Both of them glanced over their shoulders to look at Kailey. Her green eyes peeked out between their bags and her curly strawberry blond hair. She was wearing a pair of track pants that fit over her cast, and a green hoodie. "Well, Chelsey, if you want to have a nice conversation, you shouldn't bash what the other person likes."

"Ha!" Logan said.

"But I have to agree that math people aren't exactly high on the ladder of social skills."

"Ha!" Chelsey said.

"But I'm social," Logan said.

"That's just because we helped you," Chelsey answered in a know-it-all voice.

The bus pulled up just as Logan was about to reply. Chelsey ignored him and with her head held high she took his hands and slowly climbed up the steps of the bus. Logan helped Kailey out of the wagon and then locked it to the fence before throwing their stuff inside and taking his seat in the back.

After school, the twins took their place on the bottom bleachers to watch Maria play their final game of volleyball. The Bears were all over the place. Girls were missing passes and losing spikes. Coach Davis looked like he was ready to rip out his hair.

"You know," Devin said from beside Chelsey, "even though they're sucking, Mrs. Berry is still screaming her heart out. Maybe she doesn't know her daughter's a loser."

"Devin!" Kailey reached over and hit his arm.

"Well, her dad doesn't look happy," Devin said.

"He never looks happy," Chelsey said. "Except when he's watching football."

"Too bad he only had girls. No football players there," said Devin.

"Maybe one could become a cheerleader and then he could still watch football while pretending to support his daughter's cheerleading," Chelsey said.

Devin wrinkled his nose. "Can you see Kate or Leah being cheerleaders?"

"You do have a point," Kailey said. She leaned back and turned to Amanda on her left. "How was drama today?"

Amanda frowned. "Dramatic."

Kailey blinked and waited.

"Mrs. Hooper found two people making out in the supply closet."

Kailey turned back to the game. "Well, that's awkward."

"Yeah, I don't know that I would recommend signing up for drama. I guess it's good that we have dramatic people who exaggerate *everything* because they're acting, but they do it even when they aren't acting. I'll be happy when it's over."

"When is your play?"

"Just before Christmas, I think. I'm not acting. I'm doing props and stuff."

"Cool," Kailey said. "You can put all your artistic skill to good use."

Just then, Maria scored a point with a hard spike and the crowd came to their feet. The ref blew the whistle and everyone took their seats again.

Kailey looked up to see Mark standing by the door.

She nudged Amanda. "Well, look who showed up late."

"He could sit with us," Amanda offered.

Kailey smiled at her friend. Amanda was about to wave him over when he saw someone else and bounded up the steps.

"What a loser."

"Kailey!" Amanda stared at her friend.

"Well, doesn't he know that there's a row of good-looking girls right here, and off he goes to sit with some other dude—probably Al or Dan or something. Dummy."

Amanda giggled.

"What?"

"You. Perhaps I should go get him so you can deliver such sage life advice. I'm sure he would never pass up an opportunity again if he knew the way you felt."

"No, that's fine." Kailey frowned. "Stop smiling!"

"You're so cute." Amanda rubbed her back and brought her attention back to the game. The Bears didn't win. The playoffs were over for them. The girls shook hands as they departed for the dressing room. Dad came to collect his children and Amanda. Dad dropped her off and then waited to make sure she got inside before backing out the driveway.

Chelsey hit the button for the radio and immediately began to sing, "I fell in to a burning—"

"Stop!" Kailey yelled.

"Ring of fire," Devin finished.

"Please, no, I hate this song."

Dad joined his youngest two children and there was no stopping them. Kailey plugged her ears the entire way home.

CHAPTER TWENTY-TWO

"Logan? Is that you?"

Logan slowly retraced the first three stairs he'd climbed and walked into the living room. His mother sat in her favourite stuffed chair, reading by lamp light. She looked over her glasses at him and pushed her cut-across bangs out of her eyes.

"Your dad called while you were out," she said calmly.

"What does he want?"

"He wanted to see how you were doing with school, and if you would care to catch a movie or something this weekend."

Logan sat on the arm of the couch. "What did you tell him?"

"I told him I would ask and send him an email once you got home."

Logan rolled his eyes and looked across the room. His mouth remained sealed. What was his dad thinking? Of course he didn't want to meet up with him somewhere. Ray Stewart could pour as much money into his life as he wanted, but Logan had no intention of seeing him ever again. Mitch didn't mind staying with their father on the weekends, but Logan refused. He couldn't be bought.

"You need to forgive him."

He looked up and met his mother's eyes. "He's not worth it, Mom. When he walked out, he said he doesn't need to be part of our lives anymore and that's what he is to me—out, gone, and I never want to speak to him again."

"Logan..."

"I have homework," he said and abruptly left.

The twins found Aunt Louise sitting on their couch when they bustled through the door on Monday afternoon.

"Aunt Louise!" Chelsey screamed and ran to embrace her. Her boots left wet marks on the floor and her landing was softened by her large, puffy coat.

"Hey!" Aunt Louise hugged her back with a bright smile on her face. "I think you better take off all your outside clothes and come have tea with us."

Chelsey ran back to the entranceway and pulled off her hat.

Kailey come in more slowly with the aid of her crutches. She took a seat on the couch beside her aunt and leaned over to hug her. "Hi," she said, and pulled away. "Thought you'd brave the cold today and visit the land of the living?"

"It is rather cold, isn't it? Actually, your mother invited me over for tea, which is just about the only thing I can keep down." Aunt Louise smiled. "And crackers and apples."

"Good thing those are tasty," Chelsey said, plopping herself into the armchair.

Mom smiled from her place in the rocker. "How was school, girls?"

"Good," Kailey said.

"Amanda said her dog likes celery," Chelsey said. "Do you think Crazy Daisy likes celery?"

Mom raised her eyebrows. "No."

The calico waltzed in as if he owned the place. Chelsey picked him up and snuggled him under her chin. "Hello, Crazy Daisy. We were just talking about you. Do you like celery?" Crazy Daisy meowed loudly in protest.

"I think that was a no," Aunt Louise said, smiling.

"I don't blame him. Celery isn't top on my list of things to eat either," Mom said.

"Can we talk about something other than food?" Aunt Louise asked.

Kailey looked at her aunt with concern. "Sorry, Aunt Louise. How have you been feeling lately?"

"Better. I've been taking some medicine that helps me not feel like throwing up all the time. The pills have pregnant women on them."

"Seriously?"

Aunt Louise nodded with a giggle. "And they're pink."

Kailey wrinkled her nose. "Weird beard."

"No, weird pregnant lady pills," Chelsey said, and let go of her protesting cat. Crazy Daisy jumped from her owner's lap and landed on the floor. After a little shake, she stalked off to the kitchen for better entertainment. "Pregnant ladies don't have beards." Chelsey turned from watching Crazy Daisy to look at Kailey. "Well, maybe some of them do."

Aunt Louise put her hand over her mouth.

"When I worked in the maternity ward, I didn't see any pregnant ladies with beards," Mom said, picking up her crocheting again as she rocked back and forth.

"But maybe that's because they fell out. People lose hair when they have babies," Chelsey said.

Kailey glanced at her aunt; she was shaking from head to toe with her hand still over her mouth and her eyes sparkled.

"I don't think that's too likely, Chelsey," Mom said.

"Oh, well maybe they were so stressed about having a baby, they pulled all their beard hairs out." Chelsey turned and pointed a finger at Aunt Louise. "Did you used to have a beard?"

Aunt Louise snorted and then started to giggle. Kailey let out a laugh of her own, and Mom joined them in short order. Chelsey didn't understand what was so ridiculously funny.

After several minutes, Aunt Louise took a deep breath and smiled at her extraordinary niece. "No, Chelsey, I never had a beard. But if being pregnant should cause me to develop one, I will let you know."

"Oh." Chelsey cocked her head to one side and studied her aunt, then she smiled. "Thank you."

"You're welcome. So, Uncle Bruno was saying he's thinking about playing Christmas songs on the radio again."

Kailey moaned. "It's hardly even November!"

"I know, but Bruno would play Christmas songs all year round if his boss let him."

"That would be awful. No one wants Christmas all year round." Kailey rubbed an itch under her cast.

Chelsey clapped her hands. "I would! I would love to listen to them all and sing with them all and I would listen to Uncle Bruno all the time."

"Then let us all be thankful Chelsey and Uncle Bruno don't work together, or we would have Jingle Bells and Rudolf in July." Mom took the tea tray off the coffee table and walked to the kitchen.

"What time is it, Cindy?" Aunt Louise called after her.

"4:33," Mom called back.

Aunt Louise stood. "I need to be on my way, girls. Uncle Bruno still likes to eat, so I better find some canned soup for him to stick in the microwave." She winked at Kailey.

"All the food you make comes from cans?" Chelsey asked with wide eyes. "I'm going to tell Mom to buy only canned food from now on. You make *way* better food than her."

"Chelsey!" Kailey threw a pillow at her.

Aunt Louise laughed and walked to the front hallway to slip her shoes back on. "That's a lovely compliment, dear, but I don't make all my food from cans, and your mother is a wonderful cook. I only feed Uncle Bruno canned food if I'm lazy or not feeling well."

Chelsey looked concerned. "Are you not feeling well?"

"Today I'm feeling very well." Aunt Louise gave Chelsey a hug.

"It's because you have pink pregnant pills and no beard," Kailey called from the couch.

Aunt Louise laughed again. Mom came to give her a hug, and then she and Chelsey stood by the door and watched Aunt Louise get into her car. They waved her off, shut the door against the cold, and went to sit with Kailey again.

"What should we have for dinner, girls?"

"Meatloaf!" both girls said at the same time. They looked at each other and giggled.

Mom's eyes sparkled as she shook her head and finished her crochet row. "Now see what's happened? Aunt Louise talks to you for ten minutes and leaves and I'm left here with a giggle-fest."

"I really like Aunt Louise," Chelsey said once she could control herself again.

"I'm glad Uncle Bruno married her."

"Me too," said Chelsey. "He smells better now."

"Chelsey!" Kailey threw another pillow at her sister.

"What? It's true!"

"But it's not nice to say those kinds of things," Mom said. "Even if they are entirely true."

"Mom!" Kailey's mouth dropped open.

Now Mom was laughing. "Girls, I have known Uncle Bruno for a long time. When your dad and I were dating, he would only shower when he came home on the weekends from school, because his mother refused to let him sleep in her house if he was dirty. Considering that he used to play on the football team, he could get pretty smelly."

"That's disgusting," Kailey said.

"It was." Mom stood and stretched. "Come Chelsey, you want meatloaf for supper, you can mix it with your hands for me."

"Yes!" Chelsey exclaimed and followed Mom to the kitchen.

CHAPTER TWENTY-THREE

The first Tuesday of November found Logan sporting dark jeans, a brown hooded sweater, and board shoes. Gel held his brown hair in its usual style: spiked in every direction. He sniffed. *Allspice and something fruity,* he thought. *Mornings used to only smell like Allspice and the occasional wet dog.* He looked across the street and watched a shower of red and yellow leaves fall from the neighbours' trees.

Chelsey walked beside him. "This is the worst time of year ever!" she muttered under her breath. Her scowl was like a big black cloud that'd just blocked the sunshine and refused to rain.

Logan's eyebrows raised in surprise. Chelsey was almost always happy, except for last week when she told him how Devin had broken her hula-hoop by folding it in half repeatedly. He'd said he was doing strength training—his muscles against the hula-hoop. The result, however, was a broken hula-hoop with a little brother who still had weak arms. No, she hadn't been too happy about that.

"What's wrong Chelsey?" he asked, more out of curiosity than concern.

She didn't say anything, but walked along looking dejected.

Kailey answered from under all the bags on her lap. "She wants it to snow so she can make a snowman."

Three weeks had passed since Logan had first helped Kailey up the hill. It was still awkward to him, but since Kailey wasn't due to have her cast off for another three weeks, there was nothing else to do. He was just thankful he wasn't the getting pulled. It was embarrassing enough being the one at the front of the wagon; sitting in it had to be worse.

Logan looked at Chelsey. "It always snows before Christmas." He didn't know why he told her this. He didn't really care for snow. *But you do care about this girl.* The little thought surfaced, but he pushed it away.

"Really?" Chelsey looked at him with hope in her blue eyes.

He nodded. *She has huge eyeballs. She looks at me like she really believes me.*

She smiled. "Good. Then Kailey will be better and she can help."

He looked back at Kailey, whose green eyes were weary. *Chelsey's eyes are blue. Kailey's are green.* Suddenly he stopped pulling. "Oh," he said, and then continued.

"What?" both girls asked at the same time. They exchanged a confused look, then stared at Logan again.

He glanced back at Kailey, who actually looked like she wanted to know what he had to say for once. *Oh, so you* do *care about something I have to say, little Miss Stick-my-nose-in-the-air-because-I-don't-give-a-poop-about-you. Well, we'll see if I tell you or not.* "Oh, nothing," he answered nonchalantly, and got the exact reaction he was looking for.

"Yeah right!" Chelsey yelled, glaring at him.

"Chelsey, if he doesn't want to tell you, then he doesn't have to."

"Well, do *you* want to know, Kailey?" He peeked back again and saw she was struggling with his question. *Good, squirm a little.* He kept his eyes locked on her.

"What did you think, Logan?" Chelsey broke the silence. "What made you stop?"

"I'm only going to tell if Kailey wants to know."

Kailey looked from him to Chelsey and back again.

"Ask him, Kailey! I want to know! Please, *please*, ask him! I will... um...I can't really do too much—but I will think of something I can do for you."

"That's okay, Chelsey." Kailey offered her sister a gentle smile and then her voice filled with sass as she addressed their companion. "Fine. What made you stop, Logan?"

"You have different coloured eyes," he said calmly.

"I do?" Chelsey asked with real concern.

"No, Chelsey, *we* do. You have blue eyes and I have green eyes. Your eyes are both blue."

Chelsey sighed in relief.

"I actually always liked Chelsey's eyes better than mine. Blue is such a nicer colour than green."

"Well, sometimes you just need to work with what you've got," Logan said smugly.

Kailey's jaw dropped. "Thanks a lot!" She reached under the wagon for a pebble and threw it at him, hitting him in the back of the neck.

"Hey!" he rubbed his neck.

Chelsey giggled.

"Hey, whose side are you on?" Logan asked, jabbing a finger at her.

She side-stepped his attack and giggled some more. "I'm always on my sister's side. Besides, *you* were mean to her first."

Logan looked back to see Kailey smiling with a great deal of satisfaction from her place in the wagon.

"But Kailey," Chelsey chimed in. "You should be thankful you have green eyes. My eyes look like Mom's."

Kailey's face fell. "That's true Chelsey, thank you."

"What?" Logan began to ask, but the bus pulled up and both girls didn't feel like talking as he helped them up.

Lori Chanson's eyes were flashing lightning when Logan got off the bus and walked to the bike racks. He tried to slide his arm around her, but she pulled away with her arms crossed over her chest. He frowned and dropped his bag to the ground and then approached her again. She pulled farther away.

As if on cue, Kailey and Chelsey walked by with Amanda at their side.

"Look," Lori said to Logan, sass filling her voice. "It's Stupid One and Stupid Two. How on earth does anyone tell those two apart? They look and act so much alike. Are we sure they aren't both mental?"

"Why do they even go to this school?" Jeff asked, openly gawking. "Why don't they go to their own retard school like other retards?"

"Maybe they take up too much room on the short bus," Bret said. Everyone laughed. Logan joined in the laughter, and soon he felt Lori put her arm around him. He was glad. Everything was right in the world again. He leaned down to kiss Lori and then straightened to hear what joke was going to be shared next.

He caught Chelsey's eye. She had turned toward them in anger and was about to say something, but Kailey touched her arm. She whispered something Logan couldn't hear and all three girls went into the school. At the doorway, Chelsey turned for just a moment and he caught a glimpse of her downturned face.

Everything was not right in the world. His friends stood around him, laughing at the overweight boy. Logan didn't move. He felt dirty on the inside from where he stood. Chelsey had looked angry and hurt. *Just like how you feel every time Dad calls and asks about your grades and if you're on any sports teams. Never good enough. You aren't good enough, Logan. You aren't good enough for your dad, and you just hurt the one person who is trying to love you for who you are.*

Without a word, Logan pushed past Lori and took the front steps two at a time.

CHAPTER TWENTY-FOUR

Logan and Chelsey were in the same class for art. It was the second-last class before school let out for the day. Logan hated art. Art was stupid. The world didn't need any more artists, as far as he could tell; doctors, lawyers, cooks—those types of people the world could use more of. Artists, definitely not. He normally sat at the back of the class. Chelsey normally sat at the front with her friend, Amanda McGee. Today, however, Amanda was absent and Chelsey sat alone.

Mrs. Jones entered wearing a knee-length skirt, bright blue blouse, and high-heeled red shoes. "Please come up here, class. I have an announcement and some things to show you."

Logan reluctantly stood and walked to the front. No one had taken the chair next to Chelsey yet, so he slid in beside her. She ignored him, enraptured with the teacher.

"Class, the reason we do art is to express ourselves. Self-expression is extremely important for all of us, and we all express ourselves differently. Some have painted, some have sketched, some write, some act, but we all need to express ourselves. Whether you express your inner self through singing or playing hockey, you must do it. Let your inner self out."

Logan rolled his eyes.

Mrs. Jones stood still for a moment with a far-off look on her face, and then suddenly turned to her class. "Your assignment is to express yourself through paint and brush and canvas. You may paint whatever you wish, but whatever it is it must be important to you. I want it to say something about the artist behind it—to speak of who you are. We want to know what you find essential to life, something you love. Here are several examples I have brought from my home studio." She lifted a canvas from her desk and showed them. Splatters of orange, gold, red, and turquoise covered the black background. She looked ecstatic. "What do you think this says about the artist?"

The class remained silent.

"Really class, think hard."

Finally, Ben Ravenhill raised his hand tentatively. He was a shy kid with glasses.

"Yes, Benjamin!"

He ducked a little and then offered, "Maybe the artist was angry about something?"

Mrs. Jones looked disappointed. "I thought it spoke of the intense joy of light in darkness."

"Oh," said Ben, turning the colour of ripe strawberries.

Chelsey sent him a smile and Logan held in his laughter; he thought the kid was probably closer to the right meaning than their teacher. She looked like she had smelled too many markers and paint cans in her lifetime.

Mrs. Jones held up several other paintings. Some were nice and some were strange. Then she sent them to their own easels and told them to paint what was in their hearts. This project was going to take a few weeks, so if they were stuck, that was fine. There would be rough drafts and time to change your mind. She fluttered around the room, saying, "Paint what's inside you."

Logan took the easel beside Chelsey's. He glanced at her. Her face was set with determination as she took up her paints and brushes. He looked down at his. What was important to him? His father had left him, his friends were jerks. His mom was really the only one he cared about, but she would be really hard to paint. On top of that, he wasn't really certain what was inside of him, but he was pretty sure it wasn't pleasant or neat and no one would want to look at it even if he could put it down on a canvas. He thought for a moment, but his mind was a blank slate.

"Chelsey, what are you painting?" he whispered.

She jumped at the sound of his voice, then quickly turned her painting away so he couldn't see it. "Don't look!" she hissed, her eyes going around the room as if she was about to be caught for being a foreign spy.

He moved his head back. "Sure, but what do I paint?"

She turned back to her painting. "Whatever you like," she answered with a wave of her hand, then shut her mouth and that was the end of that.

Chelsey pulled her hat over her ears as they walked down the hill that afternoon. The afternoon had turned even cooler than the morning, and the wind had picked up just enough to make the weather miserable. The sun hid behind the clouds now and again as though it wanted to peek out and see what was happening below, but wasn't quite brave enough.

"Logan?"

"Chelsey."

"What's a retard, and why do your friends think me and Kailey are stupid?"

Logan was stunned to silence. That very morning, he had wondered the same thing. He'd walked away from his friends, but that hadn't really solved anything. And then he went to class and actually focused on what the teacher had been saying so he wouldn't have to deal with his feelings.

"Logan?"

He didn't look at her as he answered. "I don't know why we call you names, Chelsey. Why do you ask?"

"It makes me sad." Her answer was so soft, he almost didn't catch it before the wind snatched it away. She hugged her arms to her chest and shivered.

"Chelsey, you never said anything before." Kailey's voice held pain, and Logan wondered why they hadn't talked about it.

"Well, it makes me feel like crying," she muttered. "I just wanted to know why you call us that." She looked at Logan. "Is it 'cause we really are stupid? 'Cause I know I'm not *that* smart, but Kailey is and she's real nice, too. I think if your friends got to know her, they would change their minds."

"I don't think so. But Chelsey, we're stupid for being mean and jerks and yeah…sorry." The November breeze teased Logan's hair before moving on to a pile of leaves, scattering them around a lawn. He was glad it hadn't snowed yet; snow would make it harder to get Kailey up the hill.

"I forgive you," Chelsey whispered, but didn't utter another word the rest of the way home.

Kailey was stunned by what her sister had asked. Chelsey never talked about people being mean to her. She was amazed at the way Logan had handled it, too. *He's a donkey at school or when his friends are around, and then today he apologizes. Talk about having a split personality! I guess I should tell him thanks for talking to Chelsey, even if he is a jerk.* Kailey's mind moved a hundred miles an hour, trying to decide whether she should say anything.

Logan helped her up the front steps when they got to her house. "Thanks," she said once Chelsey shut the door.

"For what?" he asked, looking surprised.

"What you did for Chelsey. She doesn't really get it that she's…different." Kailey stood there, leaning on her crutches and feeling awkward.

"She shouldn't have to. We should give her a break." His brown eyes clouded for a minute and then they cleared. "See you tomorrow." He headed back down the steps without a backward glance.

CHAPTER TWENTY-FIVE

Dad sat in his chair in the living room after dinner. The week's paper was spread out before him. He liked news. He had always liked news. He would even change radio stations to hear the news rather than a song. It drove his family nuts, but he didn't care. They could hear the same song over and over again whenever they wanted; news was always changing and it wouldn't ever be the same twice.

"Dad?"

He glanced up to see his eldest daughter take a seat on the couch across from him. "Yes, girlie?" he answered, going back to his paper.

"Do you think God has specific plans for people? Like that He made them for a certain purpose and not something else?"

Dad folded the top-left corner of his paper slightly so he could look at her. "I think so."

Kailey nodded and looked down at her toes with a thoughtful expression on her face.

Dad laid the paper on his lap and reached for his Bible on the table to his right. "Here, I'll give you one of my favourite examples. In Exodus chapter 25, starting at verse 30, Moses is talking to the people about how they're going to build the tabernacle. He tells them God has selected two men, Bezalel and Oholiab, to teach the people what to do because these two men were filled with the Spirit and they had knowledge about craftsmanship.

"God made them for a specific purpose. I don't think when they were little they thought, *When I grow up I'll help build a place for my people to worship God.* They probably lived and learned like the rest of us do." Dad smiled at her. "So don't be discouraged if you aren't sure what to do after high school. God prepares us for our tasks and always gives us a way to complete them. You might not even know what your task was until after it's done. Life is just full of surprises like that."

Kailey smiled back. "How did you know I was thinking about after high school?"

Dad looked at his paper. "I'm just a really good dad."

"Lying is a sin."

He looked up at her again. "Hey now."

She smirked and waited.

He looked down at his paper again with a mockingly shameful expression. "I heard you talking to your mom when I came home from work."

She giggled and stood. With the help of her crutches, she hobbled over to him and leaned down to give him a kiss on the cheek. "Thanks, Dad."

He kissed her cheek in return and held her hand for a moment. "Any time, girlie."

She turned to go.

"And Kailey, God will show you what to do. So long as you live every moment before Him, you will never be disappointed in His plans for you. He has only good and rich promises for His children and He will not fail to deliver. Don't worry about the future, dear. Just live for Him now. The rest will become clear in His timing."

Kailey nodded. "Your life didn't turn out the way you expected, did it Dad?"

He let out a sigh filled with contentment and joy. "Girlie, I got far more than I could have ever bargained for. I can't count all the blessings. However, I would say you are pretty high on the list."

He watched her eyes become moist. Her lips turned up and she opened her mouth. "Love you, Dad."

"Love you, too."

He watched her shuffle away to her room to do her homework. "Yes Lord, I am very blessed indeed," he prayed. Then it was back to the news.

Mark darted around other students and headed for Kailey. He'd seen her blond head bobbing down the hallway and hurried to catch up with her. He hadn't seen her much since volleyball had ended.

"Kailey!" Mark called and bumped into another student. "Oh, excuse me," he said, reaching to set the other, much shorter person solidly on his feet, and then he hurried after Kailey again. "Kailey!"

She stopped and turned around. When she saw him she smiled and waited. *She sure is cute when she looks at me like that,* he thought. "Hey."

"Hey yourself." Her eyes were laughing. "What's up?"

"I was just wondering how you were doing?"

"Fine, I'm doing fine. How are you doing? Surviving with your bachelor uncle?"

Mark looked down at her. The top of her head stopped just under his chin. She smelled good. Not like perfume, more like soap. "My uncle's good. He's pretty easy to live with. He likes his space, but I hang out a lot with Al and Dan, so that's cool. Can I carry that for you?" he asked, seeing she had a book in her right hand and remembering what his uncle had said about carrying stuff for girls.

"Sure, I was just headed to the library to bring it back."

He looked down at it. "Shakespeare?"

"Not by choice," she said and started down the hallway again. Mark walked beside her. When they arrived at the elevator, Mark pushed the button to go down. "What are you going to do after high school, Mark?"

"I want to do something medical. That's why I came to live with my uncle. I was homeschooled, but my mom isn't so good with the sciences and she wanted me to have them under my belt before going to university. Plus, I tend to be a distracted student and I think she might have wanted me to have to listen to someone else when it comes to sitting and getting down to work."

Kailey smirked. "You realize that you'll probably need to do a lot of sitting if you want to do something medical? Just taking into consideration that school for nursing is four years."

"I did think of that. But maybe I can work in the ER."

"That would be frightening."

"Why?"

"You never know what you're going to see," Kailey said.

"That's with anything. You don't know what you're going to see when you walk down the street or into your house, either."

Kailey nodded. "I guess that's true."

Mark opened the door to the library. He put the book on the return pile and then turned to Kailey.

"I need to get another book for Geography." She started down the three steps to go to that section.

Mark followed. Shelves lined with books soon closed in around them and he began to feel claustrophobic. Books were fine, especially if they dealt with blood types and the nervous system. But shelves and shelves of books about foreign cultures where not his greatest friends. *It's now or never, or at least not for a very long time.* "Kailey?"

She looked up from her search with clear green eyes and waited.

"Kailey, I was wondering if you wanted to go out sometime? Like to a movie or get ice cream or something?"

Kailey's brain froze. *Did he just ask me out?*

"Kailey?"

She met his gaze again and said the first thing that popped into her head. "How would we get there? We both can't drive." She regretted it as soon as the words were out of her mouth.

Mark looked hurt and confused. "Well…"

"Mark." She put her hand on his arm. "I'm sorry. That was bad. That's terribly sweet of you to ask. Thank you. I'm really flattered and I like you a lot. But I'm just not into the whole dating-at-fifteen thing. I really want to be your friend. But I really don't want to date anyone till after high school. So, if it's cool with you, can we be friends for right now and hang out in groups and stuff and then maybe in three years when we are bit more grown up we can talk about it again?"

Mark slowly nodded. He looked sad.

"Mark." Kailey titled her head to look under his hanging head. When their eyes met, she spoke. "It's not 'no' forever. It's 'no' for right now."

"Okay," he said, and smiled at her.

Kailey gave him one more reassuring smile. "Besides, you have a lot of science and math to work on."

He smiled. "You're right, Kailey. Thanks. I have to go."

"Okay," she said quietly. "I'll see you later."

He waved and walked away. Kailey watched him go and sighed. *He asked me out. He likes me. Mark likes me!* Her heart beat wildly. *I probably botched the whole thing. He practically ran away after I said no, and now he probably won't ever want to talk to me again. But Dad would say we can't date till after high school anyway.* She groaned. *I guess we'll just have to wait and see.* She turned to the bookshelf and tried to remember what she had been looking for.

"Oh yes, Ethiopia."

CHAPTER TWENTY-SIX

I wonder what Chelsey would think of me dating Mark. Kailey smiled to herself. The wagon bounced and jolted underneath her. Her twin walked beside Logan, talking. Chelsey did a great deal of talking. Logan would generally mutter a response and periodically ask a question. Today Chelsey was exceptionally chatty, so Logan did mostly muttering and not too much asking. *Shall I save him from her boring story?* She waited a moment.

"Chelsey?"

Chelsey plugged her nose, making her voice sound weird, and asked, "What?"

Kailey affectionately frowned at her. "What would you say if I told you someone asked me out?"

There was a thick moment of silence before the younger of the two replied. "I'd say Daddy would beat him up and it had better not be Mark Davis because I *will* hurt him if it is!"

Kailey was stunned at her sister's violent answer. "Why would you hurt Mark if he asked me out?"

"'Cause I don't like him," Chelsey replied matter-of-factly.

Suddenly the wagon plunged to the right. Kailey screamed and grabbed the sides. She tried to lean to the left to steady the wagon and Logan pulled hard on the handle to keep her up as the back crossbar creaked and groaned under her weight. Kailey couldn't keep herself in the cart and she fell to the pavement. Hard. The right back wheel of the wagon went rolling down the street toward the park.

Chelsey screamed.

"Ow!" Kailey cried. She moaned as she rolled over to lay on the side of the road, face down in the asphalt.

"Are you dead?" Chelsey asked, staring at her sister's fallen body and clasping her hands together in fear.

Logan bent down close to her face. "You okay?" He moved his head to try and look into her eyes.

Kailey lifted her head and stared across the street at nothing. She looked at him. "No, I think I'm dead."

Logan smiled at her, a crooked smile that made his left eyebrow go up. "Does that mean I don't have to pull you up the hill anymore?"

She nodded, then put her forehead on the pavement once more.

Logan jumped up, let out a rebel yell, then looked at Chelsey. "Well, she's dead! We'll just leave her here."

Chelsey's eyes became wide saucers. Then she saw him smile. "She is not! Kailey, are you really dead?"

"Yes!" Kailey firmly replied and did not move an inch.

Chelsey looked down at her, then at Logan. "If she was dead she couldn't say yes, so you are *lying*!" She pointed an accusing finger at him and narrowed her eyes. "Now help my sister or my dad will get you good!"

"Your dad will never even know. Look, we'll roll her into that bush over there and not tell anyone." Logan bent down, ready to push Kailey's body off the street.

Chelsey stood in shock for a moment before jumping to the rescue of her sister. "*I* will tell. Now help her up!"

"Chelsey, we don't need her! She's got a broken leg and we can't use her for anything. The only thing that she does is sit in this wagon and get pulled around, which I happen to be sick of, so I say we roll her into that bush and let someone else find her. Hey, maybe that nice man who lives down the street will find her when he takes his dog for a walk tomorrow morning." Logan's face lit up at the brilliant suggestion.

"Logan, that would be awful! Poor Mr. Cho and Francis don't want find her in a bush. Besides, what will Kailey do there? No, help her up right this minute!" Chelsey put her hands on her hips.

"Why?"

"Because," Chelsey said, slightly exasperated.

"Well, when you put it like that, I guess I have to obey." He crouched down and nudged Kailey. "I'm afraid you're not dead yet, Cinderella. You'll have to come home."

Kailey waved her hand at him without looking up. "Leave me here and let me die! I've got a bum leg and now my butt's bruised; what's the point of life, anyway?"

Logan rolled his eyes, grasped her shoulders and pulled her up. "Sorry your highness, but Chelsey says you're not dead yet so you'll have to come home."

"I told you she wasn't dead!" Chelsey yelled at Logan before turning to her sister. "He wanted to roll you into a bush and leave you, but I saved you."

"Thank you, Chelsey, you're my hero!" Kailey smiled at her twin and Chelsey responded by showing all her teeth.

Logan rolled his eyes again. "Right, as if I would roll Kailey into a bush."

Chelsey pointed a condemning finger at him. "Hey, you can never be sure about people, even those you're closest to."

Well, if that isn't the truth.

Logan's thoughts were interrupted by Kailey. "How are you going to get me and the bags down the hill at the same time?" she asked.

He stood there with his arm around her for support with a thoughtful expression on his face. *I really hope Lori doesn't find out about this.* "I'll bring you two home first, then I'll come back and get our stuff." *I could leave everything thing here and just take my bag and go home. But then Chelsey will cry, really hard, and it makes me feel really bad when she cries. Besides, she still has my bike somewhere.*

"Nope, someone would have to stay here and look after our stuff. It's garbage day today," Kailey said, and he brought his mind back to the task at hand. "You and Chelsey should bring our bags home and I'll stay here and wait till you come back."

"Okay," he said with a shrug. He helped her get seated in the grass and picked up their bags. "Come on, Chelsey. We're going home."

"What about Kailey?"

"I'm coming back for her once you're home. Think you can carry that bag, Chels?" Logan asked kindly, not realizing he used her nickname.

She didn't move.

"Chelsey, go with Logan. I'll be fine right here till he comes back. Besides, you can't stay with me; he doesn't have enough hands to help the two of us."

Chelsey stuck her nose in the air, picked up a bag, then followed Logan down the hill. *Cinderella and her snooty sister,* Logan thought again suddenly. He smiled to himself all the way down the hill.

Kailey sat in the grass and waited for Logan. The garbage truck stopped and the man on the back asked if she needed any help. She politely said, "No, but you could take that broken wagon down the hill and leave it at my house." She gave him the street address and he drove away with a perplexed expression on his face. She supposed he didn't see many teenagers with bright blue casts sitting in the grass a few houses from their own home.

She turned her head when she heard someone whistling and saw Logan, hands in his pockets, walking up the sidewalk.

"Look who finally came back," she teased.

"Yeah, I should have left you here. What was I thinking? Why didn't I roll you into the bush when I had the chance?" He reached down to help her up.

"I have no idea," she answered. Logan stood on her right side and off they went down the hill toward her house.

"Did Chelsey get down the hill alright?" Kailey asked, breaking the awkward silence.

"Sure, you're the hard one to transport everywhere," Logan answered.

"Wow, thanks." Kailey would have punched him if he hadn't been her only means of getting home by dinner time. "I guess now I know how it feels to be old."

"I bet it's a nice feeling."

"Not really, but at least now I can sympathize with them."

"True." The silence stretched out between them. Kailey racked her mind to think of something to say, but Logan beat her to it. "So, *did* Mark ask you out?" He sounded unsure.

Kailey turned to him. His eyes held hers and waited. They stopped and just stared at each other in the silence. Kailey was trying to find a response. *Honesty is the best policy.* She looked away first. "Yeah, he did. Don't tell anyone, okay?"

"Why? Will your dad really beat him up?" Logan chuckled. It was a nice laugh, Kailey supposed; too bad he didn't use it more often.

"No," she said, a light coming to her eyes. "My dad wouldn't hurt anyone. He's a pretty nice guy, plus, we don't believe in beating people. But I said no and I don't want everyone to know."

"Oh," he said and remained silent.

"Does that surprise you? That I would say no to Mark?"

"I guess," he said with a shrug and started moving down the sidewalk again.

Kailey was glad when they reached her residence. He helped her up the steps with the same uncomfortable silence looming around them. "Thank you, Logan, I'll see you tomorrow," she said with a half-smile and shut the door.

CHAPTER TWENTY-SEVEN

That evening, Logan's brain just wouldn't give him peace. He kept thinking about Kailey's question as she lay on the street; what was the point to life? A lot of people just wanted happiness, but how did they get it? His father seemed to think that happiness came from money and women, but Logan knew that couldn't be true because Tom Stewart was one of the least joyful men he had ever met. He complained and moped when he didn't get his way and flew into a rage when he lost control of a situation.

His mother, on the other hand, thought happiness came from falling in love and having a family. Logan snorted. "That didn't work out either. Dad left her, I think Mitch is on drugs, and I pretty much never talk to her." Logan scratched his chin. "Maybe happiness isn't the point to life. That would explain why so many people who try to find happiness don't have a very good life." Logan turned to the dog sitting on his bed. Nog barked.

"Okay, we can go for a walk now." Logan scratched the terrier behind his ears and then snapped on the leash. Nog wagged his tail in delight. "At least I can make you happy."

He jogged down the stairs with his little friend's feet pattering after him. "I'll be back for supper, Mom," he yelled as he slipped on his shoes.

"I'd like you to barbeque some chicken when you come back," his mother called from the kitchen.

"Okay." He slammed the door behind him and was soon jogging down the street. The little terrier panted beside him, but when Logan looked down to see how Nog was doing, the dog looked up at him with his tongue sticking out of a mouth that almost looked to be smiling.

They ran in front of Mr. Smee's store just as the old man was turning his sign to CLOSED. *You should go apologize.* Logan shook off the thought and continued past the park. *It wasn't right, Logan.* He frowned. *Well it's over now, so who cares if it was wrong or right? It was months ago. He probably doesn't even remember.* He turned the corner and pulled a bit sharply on Nog's leash. *Even if he doesn't remember, you should still go in.* Nog yelped and Logan stopped to give him a break. *It's not a big deal. It's over. Done with. And if I go in alone I'll get all the blame.* Nog scratched his ear with his back foot and then stood. "Ready boy?" Logan asked. A sharp bark came in reply and they were off again. Logan put away his thoughts about Mr. Smee and whatever the point of life was. They finished the run and Logan put Nog in the backyard before turning on the barbeque.

The minute Logan saw Lori, he knew something was up. Her face was turning red and she was fidgeting anxiously with her hair. Her head popped up when he walked toward her and the emotion playing in her eyes was anything but friendly. She kept her eyes on him as he approached. He began to feel like a mouse under a feline's watchful gaze, wondering if she would play with him first or just swallow him in one foul bite.

"Hey, Lori," he greeted with what he hoped was a smile. His stomach was turning in knots trying to figure out what she was mad about this time. *She's a girl. It could be anything. Maybe I forgot our five-month anniversary…or have we been together six months? I hope she doesn't want a gift. I hate buying gifts.*

"Don't talk to me," she answered coolly and turned her head away from him with her chin up.

He looked at the guys. Bret and Jeff shrugged and Logan kept his mouth closed. It was better not to say anything in these situations than to risk saying something wrong. If he asked about the anniversary thing and it turned out to be her birthday, that could turn out very badly for him, not to mention it would be humiliating in front of everyone. No, if he stayed quiet long enough she would probably spill whatever she was mad about. *Girls are bad at keeping things inside.*

Logan looked around the school yard. The big oak that stood in the front lawn had lost most of its leaves. He pulled his jacket around him as the wind picked up. Some students stood in groups, waiting for the bell to ring. Just then something caught his eye. Mark Davis was walking with purpose toward the back door. Kailey Martin's blue jacket disappeared into the school. What she had said about Mark asking her out ran through his head. *I almost feel bad for the guy. I don't think she's interested at all. Then again, I wouldn't wish her on anyone I liked either. Not that I know if I like him or not. Chelsey doesn't like him. Though, Chelsey doesn't have very good taste in friends. She's been trying to be my friend for over a month now, and I wouldn't want me for a friend.*

Suddenly Lori whirled around to face him. "I know that you're cheating on me!" she spat at him.

Logan was stunned and quickly turned his thoughts from Kailey and Mark to the angry girl next to him. "What are you talking about?"

"You know what I mean! For over a month now you've been walking down that little hill of yours with two girls, and then yesterday you put your arm around one of them while coming home. How do I know you didn't kiss her while you were at it?"

"You mean *Kailey?* This is all about *Kailey?*" He stared at her in disbelief. *My girlfriend is jealous of Kailey Martin.* He would have laughed at the absurd thought if Lori didn't look so serious. *Kailey and I pretty much hate each other. But if Lori thinks she can boss me around, she's got another thing coming. No one tells Logan Stewart what to do.*

She slapped him. "I never want to talk to you again, Logan Stewart! If you ever come up to me again I'll have my father sue." She crossed her arms and turned her back to him.

Logan stood in shock. Not about the threat of her dad suing. That was ridiculous. He was shocked that she hit him. The group had become silent as they waited for his reaction. His cheek stung. He was about to say something about how he didn't need her anyway, that he could just pick up another girl any old time he wanted. But then he remembered something his mother taught him a long time ago when he had been mad at his brother. Whenever he was angry he was to count to five before answering. He took a deep breath and counted. *One, two, three, four, five.* He suddenly felt very tired and a peace all at once.

"Guys, I'm done with all this garbage," he said. And with that, he walked away.

Kailey didn't look up when Logan entered the classroom. She did, however, when he sat behind her and she felt the shadow. She hadn't felt the darkness for the last two weeks and now it was back. *What happened?* she wondered. Mazie was smacking her gum and muttering something about how English was right up there with Chemistry and how her grandparents never let her do anything, but Kailey didn't pay any attention to her. *He's never been nice, but in the last couple weeks he hasn't been quite so miserable. I wonder what happened.* Kailey shivered again. *Maybe I should ask.*

She turned around. "You okay?"

Logan frowned. "Mind your own business, Martin."

"Okay," she said, lightning flashing in her eyes. "Just thought you would appreciate a little concern from someone." *Once a jerk, always a jerk. I don't care what Chelsey says. I can't wait till this cast is off and I can stop asking for help from people, especially him.*

Logan hated art.

Maybe it was this pointless assignment they had to do. What was important to him? Not Lori anymore, but then when he thought about it she never really had been important to him. He had always thought he liked her, but now he realized she had been more of an accessory than a true girlfriend, whatever a true girlfriend was supposed to be like. He wasn't really sure, but he felt pretty confident that Lori wasn't good long-term girlfriend material.

I can't believe I've been dumped! I've never been dumped before in my entire life! Well, if she thinks I'm going to come crawling back to her, she can just forget it! I wouldn't go out with that cat if you paid me! Anger climbed from his heart and started to beat in his chest. He frowned and looked over at Chelsey, who was painting beside him in a world of her own; a smudge of green paint sat on her nose. *Wonder what she's painting. Better not ask. She always tells me not to look.*

He sat back in his chair and stared at the white canvass before him. *Waffles. Waffles are important to me! I eat them every morning for breakfast. I don't even like breakfast. But Mom makes me eat something and waffles are the best thing on the breakfast menu.* He wrinkled his nose. His mom usually gave him an orange, too, but he never touched it. *Now, how do I paint waffles?* He took out a brush and started. Again he glanced at Chelsey. *What's she painting?* He shook his head and started to work again.

"What happened to your face?" Chelsey asked, interrupting Logan's waffle painting.

"Huh?" Logan scrunched up his nose when he looked at her.

"You have a cut on your face and your cheek is puffy. How'd you do that?" Her big blue eyes filled with concern and her strawberry blonde locks fell around her face.

"Someone slapped me," he answered and went back to his painting. He didn't care to share the details with anyone. Lori had hit him first thing that morning and now it was almost 2:00 pm. His face had swelled up a bit, and he also had a cut across his cheek where her fingernail had sliced into his skin.

"How come someone slapped you?"

He sighed. She wasn't going to let up. "Someone didn't understand something right and got mad and slapped me," he answered with fake politeness.

Chelsey thought for a minute. "Is that like when people call me and Kailey names? Is it because they don't understand rightly?"

Logan's face was a dark mask from his eyes to his mouth. "No, Chelsey, people call you names because they're mean. It's mean to call people names. That's why it hurts."

"More than a slap?"

"Yes." He swallowed and looked away, feeling guilty.

He felt her staring at him. When he turned back to her, she was smiling. "Daddy was right."

"About what?"

"He said I had to love you even though I didn't want to. I pray for you, too. And it's getting easier because you're getting nicer!" She beamed at him and went back to work.

Logan stared at her in disbelief. *Nicer? I'm not that much nicer. I was mean to your sister this morning in English. I cheated on my human studies test. I yelled at my mom this morning. I'm not nice. And as for loving me, all you've done is hide my bike somewhere and made me walk—no, pull—you and your sister up the hill. I have this puffy face because my girlfriend slapped me because she doesn't trust me. I'm not trustworthy and I'm not nice, and if you knew what was good for you, you would stop trying to be my friend because* no one *wants to be a friend to Logan Stewart. I have nothing friendly to give and I don't need anything friendly from you.*

"What happened to Logan's face?" Kailey whispered in the darkness of their room that night. She had noticed it when they had gone down the hill that afternoon, but didn't ask because of his short reply in English that morning. Chelsey had been exceptionally quiet on the way home. Thankfully, their dad had fixed the wagon with a different tire, so Logan could still pull her up and down the hill. *Can't wait till this cast is off!* Kailey tried to scratch underneath it. *So itchy!*

"He said someone slapped him," Chelsey whispered back loudly, rolling over.

"Why?"

"Because someone was mad."

Kailey thought for a moment. "Do you know who it was?"

"Nope." Chelsey rolled over again.

"Go to sleep, girls!" Dad's voice came through the closed door.

"Goodnight, Dad! Love you more than hamsters love wheels," Chelsey hollered.

"More than mice love cheese," Kailey said.

"More than beavers love trees."

"More than rats love peanut butter."

"More than squirrels love nuts."

"More than rabbits love carrots."

"What is this? Love from the rodent department?" Dad yelled back.

The girls both smiled in the darkness and waited.

"I love you both more than porcupines love salt," Dad said.

There was silence after that declaration.

"How do you know that?" Chelsey finally asked.

"I'm smart. Goodnight."

"Goodnight!" The girls called together and waited till they heard his footsteps resound down the hall.

"Kailey?"

"Yes?" Kailey whispered back.

"Pray for Logan, okay?"

"Okay."

"I told him I pray for him, so you should pray too." Chelsey yawned. "He's getting nicer. I like him now." She sighed again and it wasn't long before Kailey heard her sister's rhythmic breathing.

"Lord," she whispered, "I need to learn to love people like you love me. I still don't like Logan and I think he's a jerk, but I guess he's one of your creatures, too, and I should pray for him. So please be with him and help him with whatever is going on in his life. And please help me to love him. Amen."

CHAPTER TWENTY-EIGHT

On Friday morning, Kailey was struggling with her locker. It was hard to balance on crutches and carry books at the same time. "Lord, maybe you could let someone stop by, so I could have an extra hand? I think I might miss my next class."

She had one textbook in her right hand and was reaching for her notebook when a voice startled her and she dropped both.

"Need a hand?"

Kailey turned to see Logan's dark figure. "You startled me," she gasped.

Logan smiled for a split second and picked up her fallen books. "What class are you going to?"

"World Geography," Kailey said and shut her locker. Logan waited for her to finish with her combination and then started walking down the hall. Kailey had no choice but to follow him. People stared at them. *Well it probably does seem weird, given past history.* Benton High students weren't used to seeing Kailey Martin and Logan Stewart walking with anyone, much less with each other. The janitor even stopped sweeping as they walked by. *Break the silence. Break the silence.*

"Thanks," she offered after a moment. "What class are you going to?"

"Trigonometry."

"Isn't that on the other end of school?"

Logan shrugged.

"Well aren't you going to be late?"

Logan shrugged again.

"You must be a sucker for punishment if you're taking Trigonometry."

Logan sent her a questioning look. "I like math."

"Oh yeah, you smell like calculators," Kailey teased. "Why do you like math?"

"I guess because it makes sense. A lot more sense than history. It's about dead people. Or Art, art is about feeling and expression. Or worse yet, the history of art. Who cares about dead people who expressed themselves?"

Kailey giggled.

"No, math is much more orderly than dead people who expressed themselves."

"Well, when you put it like that..."

"Don't you like math?"

Kailey smirked. "Let's just say I don't think math really likes me."

They rounded the corner and found Kailey's classroom on the right. She took a seat near the front and Logan put her books on the table. "Thank you, Logan."

"You're welcome." Logan turned to leave, but then stopped. "Are you going to need help after?"

"No, Maria is in my class. She should be here any minute."

"Okay," he said, and exited just as Maria walked in.

Maria entered looking confused. "Wow, Logan Stewart just smiled at me," Maria said in astonishment as she took her seat beside Kailey. "What was he doing here?"

"Helping me," Kailey answered.

"*Helping you?*"

Kailey nodded. "Maybe there are such things as miracles."

"Uncle Bruno?"

"Yes, Dev?"

"You know how we learned about spiritual gifts today at church?"

Uncle Bruno grunted from where he lay on the Martins' living room floor. Devin lay beside him. The rest of the family were scattered around the house after finishing their Sunday dinner of chicken soup.

"What do you think your gift is?"

"Wrestling."

"Seriously?" Devin's voice squeaked.

"No, though I do like a good tumble every now and again. I don't really know. Maybe being friendly. I like meeting new people. Why do you ask?"

"What do you think mine is?"

"Well, you're a kind lad, and kindness is a gift."

"I'm not always kind to Crazy Daisy. Sometimes I kick her when she's in the way. Then she meows really loudly."

Uncle Bruno stifled a laugh. "Perhaps you should work on your kindness toward cats."

"I guess."

They heard Kailey's crutches hit the floor. The thumping stopped when she entered from the kitchen, then she propped her crutches against the wall and slid onto the floor to lay beside Devin. They all lay in silence for a few minutes.

"Dev, what do you think Kailey's is?" Uncle Bruno asked.

"Telling people what to do," Devin answered immediately.

"My what?"

"How unfortunate. Perhaps she could curve that into making cookies. I think that would be more useful."

"It probably would be," Dev said.

"What are you guys talking about?"

"I'd say oatmeal cookies would be good. Made with real butter."

"And chocolate chips, not raisins. Raisins are nasty," Devin said.

"Hey now, don't be a raisin hater. What did raisins ever do to you?"

"He barfed once because of them," Kailey said.

"Really?" Uncle Bruno raised his head to look over Devin and catch her eye.

"Really."

"Well then, no raisins for you."

"Thank you," Devin said.

Dad walked in. He quietly stepped over their bodies and let himself down into his stuffed chair.

"Read to us, Daddy," Kailey said.

"Oh! Yes, please!" Devin echoed.

"I don't have a book," Dad said.

Devin sprang up in an instant and ran out of the room. He returned in short order with a book of missionary stories in hand and Chelsey trailing behind him. Chelsey sat on the couch and Devin lay down on the floor again between Kailey and Uncle Bruno.

Dad opened the book and began with the story of David Brainerd and his mission to the North American Indians. Soon Mom and Aunt Louise joined Chelsey on the couch. Aunt Louise sat down carefully due to her rounding middle. Dad read on until he had finished two stories. Uncle Bruno checked his watched and declared that 9:42 was his bedtime.

"Come along, wife," he said as he peeled himself off the rug. "You need to come home and tuck me in. We've had our story already, so all that's left to do is brush our teeth."

The Martins waved goodnight as their aunt and uncle backed down the driveway. Dad shut off the living room light and went to warm some milk in the kitchen. Mom followed and the children tromped off to the bathroom to brush their teeth.

"Who would want to drink warm milk?" Chelsey asked.

"Old people," Devin answered. Kailey tousled his hair. Their parents turned out the lights shortly after and then the house was quiet save for the wind outside.

CHAPTER TWENTY-NINE

"You know what?"

"What, Chelsey?" Kailey asked as they waited for the bus on Monday morning. Mom had driven them to the bus stop because Logan was sick. His mother hadn't said what he was sick with when she had called that morning, just that he was sick and wouldn't be able to help them up to the bus.

"When you get your cast off tomorrow, you're going to have one *really* hairy leg." Chelsey's blue eyes sparkled with laughter. Some of her hair had escaped from its elastic and was blowing in her face. She tucked it behind her ear and wiped a spot of dirt off her dark jeans.

Kailey felt her face go red. "I hadn't thought of that." The wind picked up and she held her curly hair in one hand. She was pleased with how well it was growing out. She had cut it short last year, but now it had grown out to be a few inches past her shoulders. With her other hand, she pulled her blue and white striped knit sweater down to meet her light blue jeans.

"Well, maybe you'll get a girl doctor," Chelsey said, patting her on the back as the bus drove up. One of the girls got off to help them. Kailey rolled her eyes, thankful Logan was sick and hadn't heard her sister's newest revelation.

Kailey's cast came off the second last Tuesday of November. She couldn't help grinning as the cast was cut to reveal her pasty, white skin. Chelsey had been right about it being hairy. *Maybe that's why it was so itchy. But now I can scratch it and wash it and walk up the hill all by myself!*

Mom dropped her off at school after their visit to the doctor.

"Are you sure you don't want the day off?" Mom asked. "I can always use your help with some cleaning and baking, and Aunt Louise could use a visit. She's been feeling pretty tired lately."

"Mom, I'm just so glad I don't need everyone's help anymore that I can't wait to be back!" Kailey stepped out of the car and grinned. "I'll see you at home," she said, shut the door, and limped with purpose toward the school doors.

The twins walked down the hill together, each carrying their own bags. Both were quiet. It had been six weeks since Kailey's fall; six weeks of going up and down the hill with Logan.

"I miss him," Chelsey said.

"Because now you have to carry your own bag?" Kailey teased.

Chelsey frowned at her sister. "I bet he's still sick. After we get home, I'm going to go visit him."

"If he's sick, he might be sleeping."

"Or he might be bored, because no one likes to visit sick people."

"No one likes to visit Logan regardless," Kailey said.

"But I bet he's worse when he's sick. I should go visit him so his mom can have a break. She sounds like a really nice lady when she says goodbye every morning. I bet Logan is miserable. And if he's miserable, then she's probably miserable too."

"Okay. I have a project to work on, but you can go ahead if it's okay with Mom."

"I will." They walked up their driveway and Kailey waited for Chelsey to climb the steps. She didn't moan and complain like she used to; instead, she took a deep breath and faced her fear, putting one foot in front of the other. *Logan pushed her to do that. I always help. Maybe I need to help less and make Chelsey do things on her own,* Kailey thought. Once they were both inside, Chelsey declared she was going to change her clothes and go next door. Kailey said she needed a snack and went to the fridge. She walked to the front window a few minutes later and waved to her sister as Chelsey made her way down the sidewalk once more.

CHAPTER THIRTY

Chelsey stood holding a container of cookies in one hand and with the other she held down Logan's doorbell for three seconds, then she stepped back and waited. She heard two voices inside: a deep one and a woman's, and it sounded like they were arguing. She took another step back. Footsteps sounded from inside and a moment later a stout woman with short, very curly brown hair, opened the door.

"Hi, Logan's mom!" Chelsey greeted with enthusiasm.

"Hello," the older woman said tentatively.

"I'm the girl who used to say goodbye to you every morning," Chelsey explained. She had never actually met Mrs. Stewart in person. They had been neighbours for a long time, but the Stewarts had always kept to themselves. Even when Mom waved to Mrs. Stewart when she watered flowers, Mrs. Stewart would send a very small wave back and then dart into the house.

"Oh, then you must be Logan's friend." Mrs. Stewart almost smiled then. "What can I do for you?"

"Is Logan still sick?"

"Yes."

"Can I come in and see him? Me and Mom made cookies for him."

Mrs. Stewart smiled sincerely then. "Yes, of course, do come in. I think he'll be happy to see you. Don't tell him I said this, but I think he missed you over the weekend."

"Really?" Chelsey's eyes lit up.

"Really. I'll take the cookies to the kitchen if you like, and you can take off our coat and hat and sit with him in the living room. It's just in there." She pointed across the hallway to an open doorway.

"Okay." Chelsey removed her hot pink coat and snow boots. She ducked her head in the doorway. The drapes were pulled shut and all the lights were off. The only light in the room was a yellow glow thanks to the TV screen. Logan lay on the couch. His hair was slicked back with its only natural grease and he was only wearing pajama pants. Blankets lay on the floor beside the couch, and a glass of what looked like ginger ale stood on the coffee table beside him. A thin sweat covered Logan's body. His dog lay on the floor close to his master, ready to protect him or offer his head for petting, whichever was needed.

"Aren't you cold?"

The sound of her voice caused Logan's head to rise and see who was standing in his sick room. "What are you doing here?" he asked in a none-too-friendly tone.

She came to stand before him. "I made you cookies to make you feel better," she said. "Aren't you glad?"

He moaned and let his head fall back to rest on the blue polka-dotted pillow.

Chelsey took the chair beside the couch and in front of the TV. "You look awful."

"Thanks."

"Are you bored?"

"I'm sick."

"I should bring you my favourite movies! Then you could watch them!" Chelsey's voice filled with excitement.

"That sounds like fun," he muttered sarcastically.

"Aren't you going to ask what my favourite movie is?"

"What's your favourite movie?" he asked, looking from her to the door that led to the kitchen. He hoped his mother hadn't eaten any of the cookies Chelsey had brought, because he was quite doubtful in regards to her baking abilities, and he still needed his mother for a while.

"I like Snow White and the Seven Dwarves," she said.

He grunted and closed his eyes.

"If you were one of the Dwarves, you would *not* be Happy," she said defiantly.

He sent her a dark look and then sneezed. "I'd be Sneezy." He reached for the tissue box on the coffee table.

"No," Chelsey said with certainty. "You would be Dopey."

Logan was about to share what exactly was on his mind, but he started coughing and by the time he was done he decided not to bother.

Chelsey stayed for an hour. She talked. She talked about everything—how school was, that they missed him walking with them, that Kailey's cast was off and her leg was hairy—but she told him not to tell Kailey she had said that. She told him to turn off the bad shows twice. He didn't want to comply, but she gave him such a look of shame that in his weakened condition he couldn't argue.

"If you're still sick tomorrow, I will bring over some movies," she told him as she got up to leave.

"Great." He waved as she walked out the door.

His mother entered with a plate of cookies.

"Are those from Chelsey?" Logan asked.

"Yes."

"I don't care what you do with them, just don't let anyone eat them. It will probably be the last thing they do." With that he rolled over and tried to fall asleep, hoping he'd be better tomorrow so he wouldn't have to watch *Snow White*.

But he wasn't better. In fact, by the time Chelsey arrived the next day, videos in hand, he had blown his nose so much that it had rubbed raw and his head felt like it was going to explode. His eyes had bags under them due to lack of sleep. He blinked while she placed three movies on the table: *Snow White, Sleeping Beauty,* and *Beauty and the Beast*. He was just thankful that she hadn't brought any more cookies.

"Which one?" she asked, hands on her hips.

He shrugged. "You said you liked *Snow White* best, so put that one on." He pulled the blanket under his chin and watched her put the movie in. His sleep-filled eyes watched the wicked queen ask the mirror who was the fairest in all the land, and the huntsman take Snow White deep into the forest to cut out her heart. A movement caught his eye.

Chelsey had her hands over her eyes so she couldn't see.

"What are you doing?" he asked.

"I don't like this part," came the muffled reply.

"Why not?"

"It's scary."

"He doesn't cut her heart out." Logan sniffed, tilting his head to the side. Lori's sisters had been watching this part once when he came to pick her up for a date.

"I know." She moved her fingers so she could see through the slits they made. "Is it done yet?"

Logan looked at the TV. "Yeah, it's done."

She put her hands down, grinned, and turned back to the movie. When the witch appeared before her mirror again, Chelsey's hand flew to her eyes. She asked Logan to inform her when it was over. After the third time Logan told her it was alright to look again, she turned to him. "Why aren't you scared, Logan?"

"Well, someone had to be willing to watch the scary parts, or who would tell you when it's safe to look again? If we both closed our eyes, we would spend the entire movie with our eyes closed and then we might as well not watch it at all. Who usually watches this with you?" He coughed.

"Kailey, but she likes *Cinderella* best. It has less scary parts."

"Then why didn't you bring that one? You can look again."

She put her hands down and turned to him. "Because we broke it when it fell down the stairs, but that was a long time ago." Her eyes went to the TV.

"Why did it fall down the stairs?"

"We were fighting over it."

"Oh, I see." Logan smiled to himself. Their visit continued through the movie. Chelsey kept putting her hands over her eyes and he continued to let her know when it was safe to look again. He almost enjoyed it. It was nice having someone to look out for.

"Hurray!" Chelsey cheered when the prince came and broke the spell that held Snow White.

Logan put his hands over his eyes.

"What are you doing?" Chelsey asked in bewilderment.

"I don't like this part," he said through his hands.

Chelsey turned back to the TV. "You can look."

Logan looked. "Ew!" He put his hands back over his eyes.

"Hee, hee, I tricked you, they weren't done kissing yet!" she exclaimed and clapped her hands.

"Thanks a lot! How can you watch that part?" Logan reached for another Kleenex.

"'Cause I'm a girl, and boys might be braver when it comes to cutting out people's hearts, but girls are *way* braver when it comes to kissing!" She giggled.

Logan could have begged to differ, but he kept his mouth shut and watched Snow White bid farewell to her band of little dwarves. After the movie, Chelsey went home for dinner but left the fairy tales behind with Logan, just in case he wanted to watch them. Logan smiled to himself as he fell asleep.

CHAPTER THIRTY-ONE

The next morning, Kailey stood beside Chelsey as they waited before Logan's front door. Chelsey held the doorbell down for three seconds and then stood back and waited. Kailey was wearing her favourite dark skinny jeans, tall brown boots, a large knit burgundy sweater, light brown scarf, and black coat. It was nice not to be wearing track pants. She adjusted her headband around her ears and rubbed under her eyes to remove any make-up that may have smudged. She watched Chelsey tap her foot. Impatient.

Logan's mom stuck her head out the door. "Good morning, girls. Come on in. Logan will be right down." She opened the door wide for them.

"Good morning, Logan's mom. How are you today?" Chelsey asked.

"I'm fine, thank you."

"This is my sister, Kailey. We're twins."

"I can see that. It's nice to meet you, Kailey," Mrs. Stewart smiled.

"You too, Mrs. Stewart." Kailey shook the older woman's hand. "We just stopped by on our way to the bus to see how Logan was, but I guess he's well enough to go to school." Kailey had hoped that he wouldn't be up to the trip up the hill with them.

"I think Chelsey's movies are what did it." Mrs. Stewart whispered as though she was sharing a confidential, international secret.

Just then Logan walked down the stairs.

"Good morning!" Chelsey greeted with a grin.

"Good morning. Hey, Kailey."

"Hey, feeling better?"

Logan nodded. "You got your cast off." He dumped his bag on the floor, reached for his coat, and pulled on his shoes.

"You three have a good day at school today," Mrs. Stewart called as she headed back to the kitchen.

"Bye, Logan's mom!" Chelsey called after her.

"Bye, Chelsey."

Chelsey sent Logan a frown and waited.

He sighed. "Bye, Mom."

"Bye, Mrs. Stewart!" Kailey yelled after him and opened the door.

"Bye!" Mrs. Stewart yelled from the kitchen as they all exited the house.

Logan shut the door behind them. He pulled Chelsey's backpack on and shouldered his own knapsack.

"Kailey can play in the snow! Her cast came off!" Chelsey walked in between them, holding Kailey's hand as they climbed the hill.

"But there's no snow yet," Logan answered.

"But someday there will be." Chelsey eyes lit up at the thought. "And when that day comes, we can all play in the snow together and build the biggest snowman in the entire world. Then we'll be famous."

"I don't want to be famous," Kailey said.

"Okay, then you can sit at home and watch us on TV, and Logan and I can be famous."

Walking up the hill with the twins didn't bother Logan as much as it once had. Between sleeping and taking medication, he had thought about them. It was foolish for people to make fun of Chelsey simply because she was different. He wasn't going to do it anymore. She wasn't his friend, but she also wasn't his enemy. The twins were not his ideal people to hang out with, but it was okay walking to the bus with them. He wasn't sure how to sort out his thoughts on the matter. On one hand he was cool—far cooler than they were—but on the other hand they had something that he thought he wanted. He just didn't know what it was, exactly.

"Bus is here!" Chelsey cheered when they got to the top of the hill.

Logan took their bags into the bus without a thought and put them down. He turned to help Chelsey, but Kailey was already holding her hands. "Thanks anyway, Logan." She smiled, helping her twin sit down. Logan nodded and went to the back.

CHAPTER THIRTY-TWO

Chelsey walked beside Logan on the way to the bus stop on Tuesday morning. "Logan?"

"Yes, Chelsey?"

"Will you come to our Christmas program at church and listen to me sing?"

"No," he answered shortly.

"Why not?"

"Because I don't go to church."

"Well, that's dumb."

"Why?" He turned to her.

"Because church is important," she answered. "And you should come because you need church."

"Do not."

"Yes, you do, 'cause everyone needs church." She stuck her nose in the air. "Unless you're scared of church. No one will hurt you there, Logan. Everyone is real nice! Well, except Mr. Jeffery. He's old and frowns a lot. But Uncle Bruno says he has a good heart. Everyone else is friendly."

"Chelsey, I don't go to church."

"I dare you," she said curtly.

He growled under his breath and didn't answer, ending the conversation.

Kailey wisely remained silent through the exchange. Logan wasn't going to come to church. Why would he? They weren't his best friends, and he didn't like church, so why would he combine two things he didn't like? That would be like mixing hot peppers and fish.

Logan threw their bags onto the bus and walked to the back.

"I wouldn't count on him coming, if I were you," Kailey told her sister.

"But you aren't me," Chelsey said in total confidence, and turned to start talking to Mrs. Brown, the bus driver.

Chelsey was quiet on the way home on Wednesday. She walked between Logan and Kailey with a sorrowful expression on her usually happy face. Halfway down the hill, Kailey turned to ask her sister how her art project was coming along when she saw a big tear make its way from Chelsey's right eye down her chin. Kailey stopped and touched her sister's arm.

"Chelsey, what's wrong?"

Chelsey looked up at her sister and sniffed. "Roger died."

Kailey racked her brain, but she couldn't think of anyone named Roger. "Who's Roger?"

"Mrs. Brown's grandson. He had cancer." She sniffed again.

Kailey quietly took her twin into her arms. Chelsey's head rolled against Kailey's shoulder and her tears soaked Kailey's coat.

"He was only twenty-four," Chelsey choked as she moved her head back to look in Kailey's eyes. "That's really young. He was going to get married. Why did he have to die?"

"I don't know, Chelsey. All I know is that God knows best," she wiped her sister's tears with her mitted hand. "Think you're okay to walk home? We can talk about it with Dad when he gets home."

Chelsey nodded. Kailey took her hand and they walked home. Logan waved goodbye when he turned to his driveway. Kailey waved back, but Chelsey was still sniffing beside her.

Kailey took up running again nearly as soon as her cast was off. It had taken some time for her to build her strength up again. As soon as they got home, she changed into her sports clothes, pulled her tuque over her ears, and slipped out the door. She ran down the street for her normal route. She passed Mr. Smee's store and waved to the shop owner. It was almost 4:30. He would be closing up soon.

Her thoughts turned to Mark. He bumped into her in random hallways and they weren't even in any of the same classes. She wasn't sure if she should hint to him that they couldn't be together for the next three years, so he might as well cool it. She shook her head. That would be rude. A smile snuck up on her face. She could just tell Chelsey about it. Then he would cool it in a hurry.

The wind blew in Kailey's face as she ran, nipping her nose and cheeks. The sun set in red with streaks of gold, as if crying for attention from the people down below. It was the last day of November. Along with saying goodbye to that month came saying hello to snow, colds, and Christmas. The sound of a dog's bark startled her and she looked toward the park.

A little brown, black, and white terrier came running toward her. She looked up just as something hit her in the head. She touched her head and looked down to see a ball roll away. She picked it up. The terrier stood before her, shaking its tail in delighted anticipation. She crouched to pet the little fellow while rubbing her head where the ball had hit her. "Is this what you want, boy?"

The dog's entire body wiggled and he barked, waiting for her to throw it.

"Sorry about that, Kailey. I didn't see you there."

Kailey looked up as Logan sauntered toward her. "Hey, so this is the dog that barks in your backyard."

"Yeah." Logan shrugged.

"What's his name?"

"Nog."

Kailey gave him a skeptical look. "Where'd you get a name like that?"

"It's kinda dumb."

"I live with Chelsey. Nothing surprises me anymore."

"My mom played the song *In the Land of Nod* and I liked the song, but I like the name *Nog* better than *Nod*, so I named him after that. But you don't have to spread that story around."

She stood. "Oh, of course not. I wouldn't dream of saying anything to anyone." Her eyes sparkled. "I should go. Mom wanted me home for supper."

"I should go, too." Logan put the leash on Nog. "Since I nailed you in the head with a ball, I guess I better make sure you get home okay."

Kailey wasn't sure what to do with that offer. She didn't really want to walk back to her house with Logan Stewart. *But maybe he just needs someone to talk to.* "What am I going to do? Walk into the street and get hit by a car or something?"

"You never know," he answered, and started walking toward their houses before she could refuse him. She followed his lead in silence. "How's your leg?" Logan finally asked.

"Oh, good," Kailey answered in surprise.

"I bet it's less itchy now that the cast is off...and maybe a little less hairy." He winked at her.

"Who have you been talking to?"

"A little bird."

"Chelsey." Kailey shook her head.

"Speaking of Chelsey, has she talked much about Roger dying?"

Kailey was startled by the question. She hadn't thought he cared much about how Chelsey felt. "She was talking to Dad when I left."

Logan kept quiet. Kailey stole a look at him.

"She'll be okay. Dad is good to talk to."

Logan's head bowed in a slight nod.

"Can I ask you something personal? You don't have to answer," she asked as they turned the corner.

"Sure."

"Um...why haven't I seen you with your old friends lately?"

"They're jerks."

"Oh." She watched Nog trot along in front of them.

"Kailey, you don't have to be nice about it. We both know they were good-for-nothings and I'm better off not hanging with them. Besides, what do you care? You don't even trust me."

"Maybe you should give me a reason to trust you," she shot back.

"Maybe you shouldn't be so defensive!"

"Defensive? I think I have every right to be defensive, since you've been mean to Chelsey and me for as long as I've known you. You've called us names and laughed at us. I'm surprised you didn't do some kind of bodily harm to one of us. Really, Logan, we have no reason to trust you."

By this time they had made it to Kailey's laneway. They turned to face each other and Nog took a seat at his master's feet.

"Maybe I'm different," Logan said in a forcibly controlled voice.

"Maybe you should prove it. Trust is earned."

"Fine!"

"Fine!" she shouted back and spun on her heel. She marched up the front steps, went into the house, and slammed the door.

CHAPTER THIRTY-THREE

"You missed out on a really good Christmas program, Logan," Chelsey said glumly as they trudged up the hill.

Logan grunted. *I told her I don't like church. I told her I don't go to church.*

"Logan, you would have liked it. You pretend you don't like anything, but I know you would have liked it. I sang and it sounded good."

"He likes math," Kailey offered.

"Okay, you pretend you don't like anything other than math, which is weird. You're weird."

Logan frowned at her.

"And grumpy. Why are you always grumpy?"

"I'm not grumpy."

"Well you sure look and sound grumpy." Her face filled with a stubborn determination.

"My mom is going away tonight, so I won't have anything to eat."

"You can't cook *anything?*" Kailey's eyebrows rose.

"Do you want to come over for supper?" Chelsey asked.

"No."

Chelsey cocked her head to one side. "No you can't cook anything, or no you won't come over?"

"I can barbeque and make grilled cheese. And I'm not coming to your house."

Chelsey shook her head. "How did you get to be this old and only know how to barbeque?"

"Well, what can you cook?"

"Noodles and pizza and toast and potatoes and eggs and orange juice and—"

"Chelsey, you don't cook orange juice," Logan interjected.

"How would you know? All you know how to do is barbeque." Chelsey wore a smug expression on her face.

Logan frowned.

Kailey rolled her eyes.

"So," Chelsey said, breaking the silence. "Supper is at 5:30. You can wear whatever you want."

"Chelsey, I don't want to come."

"Well, sometimes you need to do things that you don't want to do. And eating with us is better than starving. I think Uncle Bruno and Aunt Louise are coming, too. You'll like them." Chelsey shared a big smile with him. The bus pulled up.

At 5:28, Logan stood on the Martins' front step and rang the doorbell. He didn't need to wait long. The door opened, showering him with light.

"Come in, Logan." Kailey held the door open for him. He stepped past her into the entranceway. She took his coat and hung it up and he pulled off his shoes. It sounded like a lot of bumping and grunting was coming for the room to his left. He looked at Kailey with confusion, and to his surprise she smiled. "Uncle Bruno and Aunt Louise are here. Uncle Bruno likes to wrestle."

Chelsey screamed.

"Come and see." Kailey led the way through the open doorway to a large living room. On the floor, a big man with red hair lay pinned by Chelsey and a boy of seven. "Guys, Logan is here."

With Kailey's announcement, all their heads flew up. In the next moment, Kailey had disappeared and Logan found himself lying on the floor with the big man sitting on his chest and Chelsey leaning into his face.

"Hello Logan," she said with sparkling eyes. "We're going to tickle you." With that, he felt someone touch his feet and he did what would be anybody's first reaction. He kicked. Pushing the big man off of him, he grabbed the little boy, who had been holding his left foot. He heard Chelsey yell and then felt her collide into him. Logan tried desperately to get away, but Chelsey and the boy had practice. The big man sat on the floor and watched them for a moment before joining in the chaos. Sometimes he helped Chelsey and sometimes he helped Logan; most of the time he just laughed.

"Dinner time, warriors."

Logan looked up. Chelsey was hanging on his back and the boy was pulling on his leg. Another man with graying dark hair stood in the doorway to the kitchen. He was wearing a checkered blue and white shirt and jeans. Chelsey got off Logan and the boy stood.

"Hurray! Supper!" Chelsey cried and walked past the man.

He smiled and held out his hand. "You must be Logan. I'm Bill Martin. I see you've already met my son, Devin, and this is Bruno Cowden."

Logan shook his hand.

The big man with red hair slapped him on the back. "You can call me Uncle Bruno." He looked at Mr. Martin and pointed to Logan. "I like this kid. He fights well. Come on Devin, we better go wash our hands, or Aunt Louise won't let us eat anything."

Logan followed them to the bathroom and then to the kitchen.

"Hello, Logan. I'm Cindy Martin, and this is Louise—she's married to Bruno."

Logan shook the hands of both women.

"You can sit between Chelsey and Dev," Mrs. Martin said, pointing across the table.

Logan took his seat. Devin poked his arm and handed him the water jug. "Can you pour some for me, too? It's too full for me." Logan nodded and poured a glass for him before filling his own. Chelsey slid into her seat next to him and quickly passed him her glass as well.

"Shall we pray?" Mr. Martin asked. The entire family bowed their heads. Logan followed suit. "Dear Heavenly Father, we thank you for this day that we could work and go to school. Thank you that Bruno and Louise and Logan can all be here to join us. Thank you for this food, and please bless it to our bodies. Amen."

Logan looked up.

"What's for dinner?" Mr. Martin asked.

"Chelsey asked for spaghetti." Mrs. Martin stood to serve the noodles. "Devin, you can pass around that garlic bread. Do you like spaghetti, Logan?"

"Yes, thank you." Logan took his plate back from her. Devin passed the bread. It smelled good. Logan wondered if there might be something with apples in the oven, since the air had a mix of tomatoes, garlic, and cinnamon.

"How have you been feeling, Lou?" Mr. Martin asked.

"Better."

"Aunt Louise is going to have a baby," Chelsey whispered to Logan.

He nodded. *Would have never guessed, since her stomach is an odd, round shape.*

"I'm doing better, too. A man can only live on fried eggs, burgers, and frozen pizza for so long. Though I think I could live longer on burgers than fried eggs." Bruno bit into the garlic bread.

"Good thing you don't have a sick wife," Chelsey said to Logan, "because you wouldn't eat anything."

Devin turned and stared at Logan. "You can't cook anything?"

Logan opened his mouth. "I can cook."

Chelsey put down her fork. "What? What can you cook?"

"Cereal. Waffles. I can barbeque."

"Cereal is not cooking."

Logan looked at her. "This from the girl who said that she could cook orange juice."

Chelsey put more noodles into her mouth.

"Where did your mom go, Logan?" Kailey asked, changing the subject.

"I don't actually know. She said she'd be back later tonight." Logan rolled his spaghetti onto his fork.

"Chelsey, did you like all the Christmas songs we've been playing at the radio station?" Uncle Bruno asked.

Chelsey's eyes grew in excitement. "Yes!"

"I think you could play a few more carols and a few less about Santa and Rudolf," Kailey said.

"What are you, a reindeer hater? Santa isn't going to bring you any gifts if you bash all the songs about him. How would you like it if someone heard this song: *Kailey Martin she's just so sweet, Kailey Martin is the girl to meet, Kailey Martin, oh oh oh,"* Bruno sang to his own tune. "And then they bashed it and were like 'could you please stop singing about Kailey? She's not even for real.' How would you like that?"

"I'd probably jump out at them from behind something and scare them. Then they would know I'm real."

"I'm going to talk about you on the radio tomorrow."

Kailey groaned.

"You need to be careful what you say around Uncle Bruno, because he's always looking for something to say on the radio," Chelsey whispered loudly again to Logan.

"It's because radio hosts aren't funny on their own; they use humor from other people to make their jokes," Mr. Martin said. "I wonder who had the bright idea to give Bruno a microphone in the first place."

"Probably a deaf man," Mrs. Martin said.

"Hey now!" Bruno objected.

"Would anyone like some more? Logan?"

He shook his head.

Bruno took seconds. The conversation continued until Mr. Martin took out a Bible and read a passage about Jesus healing a blind man. The family discussed how the Pharisees didn't believe, and how they were just as blind as the blind man had been. Mr. Martin asked Devin to pray, so they all bowed their heads and listened to him pray. Mrs. Martin shooed them into the living room so she could clear the table. Shortly after they took their seats, Kailey arrived with a tray loaded with pie, ice cream, coffee, and tea. She served them all and then went back to the kitchen.

Logan was going to leave after dessert, but Chelsey asked him to stay and play a trivia game with the rest—otherwise they wouldn't have even teams. Logan joined the team with Chelsey, Mr. Martin, and Aunt Louise. Kailey, Uncle Bruno, Mrs. Martin, and Devin made up the other team. The teams were fairly even with Bruno's knowledge of random things thanks to working at the radio, and Logan's documentary obsession. In the end, Logan's team won and Bruno announced that they would need a rematch very soon.

Logan walked home with a warm feeling inside. He opened the door and Nog ran to greet him. "Hey, little guy." He scratched the dog behind the ears and then climbed the stairs to bed. Nog trailed behind him. Logan yawned. He brushed his teeth, changed into his track pants, and fell into bed. Nog curled up at his feet.

CHAPTER THIRTY-FOUR

Chelsey pulled herself out of bed on Thursday morning. She stood and stretched her arms out as far as they would go until she felt something crack in the middle of her back. She nodded with satisfaction and glanced at the top bunk to see that Kailey was already up. *Probably in the shower.* Smacking her lips, she walked toward the window and opened the blind. All sleep fled from her eyes. It took a second for the sight before her to sink in. Then she screamed.

"It snowed! It snowed!" She danced in a circle and squealed, then ran out the door to the kitchen, slipping in her socked feet. "Mom! Mom! Look out the window! It's the first snowfall! And there's like a foot of it!" Chelsey hugged her mother and then stood next to the window with a look of pure delight.

"I think it's closer to about two inches, honey," Mom said.

"It's beautiful!" Chelsey sighed. She spun on her heel and looked her mom in the eye. "I'm going to go change and build a snowman!"

"You have school today."

Chelsey froze. "Isn't it a snow day?"

Mom smiled gently. "No. They had the roads plowed by the time Dad and I got up." Mom picked up her coffee cup again and took a sip.

Chelsey's body sagged and she walked back to her room to get ready for school. Kailey found her there a short time later, her head stuck in her sweater. Kailey helped pull it down the rest of the way and out pooled Chelsey's frowning face.

"What's up, cute duck?" Kailey asked.

"It snowed."

"Haven't you been looking forward to snow since last Easter?"

"Mom says I have to go to school."

"Well, we could tie Mom up and play outside instead," Kailey suggested. Chelsey was about to respond but Kailey beat her to it. "But then Logan would need to walk up the hill all by himself, and Mom probably wouldn't make us any lunch or supper, so maybe I should braid your hair for you instead."

Chelsey's eyes shone again. "Okay, I like it when you braid my hair."

An orange towel kept Kailey's hair on the top of her head while she worked on her sister's wild locks. Once she was finished, Chelsey went back to the kitchen to get breakfast. As she walked down the hallway, she heard the blow-dryer.

It was a long day for Chelsey. She talked about the snow when they walked up the hill. She sat in class, longingly looking out the window. At lunch time she couldn't really build anything because she wasn't wearing her snow pants. She perked up on the way down the hill, chattering the entire time about how happy she was that it had snowed.

"Come on Kailey, let's go build a snowman," Chelsey announced from the doorway. The only distraction she'd had upon arriving home was the fresh batch of oatmeal cookies Mom produced just as they walked in the door. Now she stood wearing her snow pants, tuque, and scarf.

Kailey looked up from the table in the living room. "Chelsey, I'm really sorry, but I have to work on this project. It's due next week Tuesday and I have a lot of work to do on it yet. Maybe ask Devin?"

"He's no fun. Can you please come out?"

"No, I'm really sorry."

Chelsey's bottom lip started to curl out. "Will you at least zipper up my coat so I can put my mittens on first?"

Kailey smiled. "I'd be happy to." She stood and zipped up the hot pink coat, tucking Chelsey's scarf securely inside and pulling her hat on so only her eyes and the tops of her cheeks showed.

"You'll be sorry you missed this," Chelsey muttered through her scarf.

"Bye, Chelsey!" Kailey waved and shut the door before turning her attention to her biology project.

"Please!"

"No!" Logan insisted to Chelsey, who was standing outside before him on his top step. He had just managed to take off his coat and boots before going to the fridge when the doorbell sounded for three seconds. Now he stood in the entranceway in his socks with a cup of milk in one hand and a chocolate chip cookie in the other.

"Please, please!" she begged. "Kailey's got a big project to do, so she can't come outside."

"No! I have better things to do than play in the snow."

"Is it because you don't know how? I can teach you, don't worry!" Chelsey's voice filled with hope.

"I know how to make a snowman. I just don't want to." He bit his cookie.

Chelsey stuck her nose in the air. "No. I bet no one ever showed you how when you were little, did they? And now you're too proud to try."

Logan growled and shut the door.

The doorbell rang for three seconds. He pretended not to hear it and started to go upstairs.

"What does Chelsey want?" his mother called from her office. "She won't stop ringing the doorbell."

"I'll go tell her to stop.," Logan went back down the stairs. He put the rest of the cookie in his mouth and opened the door. Chelsey stood waiting. "Stop!" he commanded, and was about to shut the door but she stuck her hand out to stop him.

"Please come out and play with me. Otherwise I won't tell you where I hid your bike." She crossed her arms to show him she meant business.

"Chelsey, I think it's about time you gave me my bike back. I walked up the hill with you, which was the original deal."

"Not if you don't come play outside."

"If you don't leave me alone, I won't walk with you anymore," Logan said. That was good threat. She liked it when he walked with them.

"Yes you will. Who else is going to walk with you? I still have your bike." Chelsey wrinkled her nose.

Logan groaned in exasperation. "What about Devin? Doesn't he want to play?"

"Devin has a cold. Kailey gave it to him."

"Kailey hasn't had a cold."

"Well, do you want your bike back or not?"

"Chelsey, has it ever occurred to you that I do a lot more for you than you do for me?" he asked with forced patience.

"Yes, but did it ever occur to you that you can do more stuff than I can?"

"Fine. I'll be out in a minute." He shut the door in her face. Finding his snow pants, he yelled to his mother before he went out. "I'm going to go build a snowman; that's what Chelsey wanted. Bye!" And with that, he slammed the door behind him.

Kailey was deep in thought and study about how the liver worked when she heard the front door open. *Chelsey must have gotten cold.* She jumped when a deep a voice asked, "Do you have a carrot?"

Kailey glanced up and the sight before her shocked her into silence. Logan stood just inside the doorway wearing a long tuque, like an elf's hat, snow pants, a coat, mittens, and a scarf. His brown hair stuck out from under his tuque and his eyes were bright. His breath was slightly laboured. The cold air that had blown in with him made her shiver.

"It's for a snowman," he informed her with a roll of his eyes.

"Oh," she said. "Ask Mom."

He didn't look at her twice but yelled, "Hey, Mrs. Martin! Do you have a carrot?"

"Chelsey suckered you into playing with her, eh?"

Logan nodded. Mom came from the kitchen wearing an apron and bearing a carrot. She handed it to him. He pulled his scarf down the reveal his mouth. "Thanks," he said, and then went back outside.

Mom turned to Kailey and both ladies shrugged before going back to their activities. Logan came back in several times—asking for an old pot, then another carrot, and last of all two old scarves. Finally her curiosity got the better of her and Kailey went to look out the window. What she saw made her smile.

In their front lawn sat three balls of snow, one on top of the other, and on the top sat a pot with the handle sticking out to one side. An old red scarf was around its neck, flapping slightly in the breeze. He wasn't an exceptionally large snowman, thanks to the lack of snow, but he was still there, proudly standing in their yard. She started to laugh. "Mom, come look."

Mom came up behind her. "What?"

Kailey pointed.

Mom smiled. "That's good. You should take some pictures. I'll get the camera."

Kailey's mouth curved up as she watched Logan and Chelsey roll balls in his front lawn; a large one was ready for the next two, and a scarf and carrot lay on the front steps, waiting to be put in place.

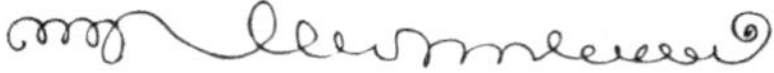

Logan stepped back to survey their second snowman. "He looks pretty good."

"Think he's cold?"

He rotated to look at Chelsey. "He's a snowman. If he wasn't cold, he'd melt and die."

She kept looking at the snowman. "Yeah, I guess."

They stood and looked at their masterpiece as a car pulled into the drive. "Oh no," Logan muttered under his breath.

"Who's that?" Chelsey asked, squinting at the tinted windows to try and make out who was inside.

"My brother. I think you should go home now." Logan watched Mitch emerge from his car. He was tall with blond hair and a shaggy beard. He was wearing a leather jacket and from where Logan stood he thought he smelled a hint of marijuana.

"Why?"

"He's not nice," Logan answered and turned to her. "Come on, I'll walk you back." He reached for her hand without thinking and began to walk toward the sidewalk.

"Who's your friend, Logan?" Mitch yelled.

Logan ignored him.

"That's your brother? He doesn't look like you."

"You should stay away from him."

"Why you kids leaving so soon? I could help with your snowman." Mitch laughed in a deep and unfriendly sort of way.

"Go jump on a landmine, Mitch," Logan yelled over his shoulder, leading Chelsey away from his brother. He helped her up her steps.

"That wasn't very nice. How come you don't like him?" Chelsey asked.

"Because he's a jerk."

"You were a jerk," Chelsey pointed out.

"Yeah well, not near as bad as he is."

Chelsey didn't answer. She opened the door and stepped inside. "Thanks for playing with me today. Devin doesn't really have a cold; I just don't like playing with him as much as I like playing with you. Bye," she said and shut the door.

"Bye." Logan trudged back to his house, wondering how long Mitch would be staying this time.

CHAPTER THIRTY-FIVE

"What? Why?" Logan's eyebrows met above his nose and his mouth turned upside down.

"Because I have to. Your aunt just had a baby and she needs a hand." Mrs. Stewart sat at her desk. She shut her laptop and slid it into its case. Pens, calculator, sticky notes, and two binders followed.

"Don't call her that!" Logan placed his hands on either side of her desk and leaned in, his face close to hers.

"Logan," his mother began, her voice quiet and sad.

"No, she's Dad's sister so she is not my aunt."

"Logan." Her voice remained quiet but became firm. "Just because your father has turned his back on his family does not mean that we will, too. I'm going. Mitch is going to stay here while I'm gone."

Logan slammed his fist on the desk and turned around to face the window.

"You two will be just fine."

Logan sent her a skeptical look over his shoulder.

"You just need to try harder." She picked up her notebook. "There's food in the refrigerator for supper. Just heat it in the microwave." She looked at her watch. "You better get going; the girls will be here shortly."

Logan sighed heavily and made for the door.

"And Logan..."

He turned.

"I'll be back Saturday afternoon. I'll only be gone two nights. You'll be fine."

"Wanna bet?" he retorted and stalked away.

"This is beautiful, Chelsey," Mrs. Jones handed her back the painting. "I love it, really. Have you ever thought about studying art after high school? You have natural talent, and you could really grow in a full-time art program. This painting is already so original, creative. I sincerely think you could sell it."

"No." Chelsey shook her head. "I could never sell it. It's for something special."

"Fair enough." Mrs. Jones smiled. "May I ask why you painted it that way?"

Chelsey scratched her head and studied her shoe, then looked back up at her teacher. "I guess that's the way I see it in my head."

The bell rang.

"I have to go to the special ed room now."

"Okay. Thank you, Chelsey."

Chelsey waved goodbye to her teacher as she walked out of the class.

"Don't let Chelsey come over tonight," Logan whispered to Kailey on Friday morning before English class. The previous night with Mitch had been uneventful. Logan had microwaved his dinner and fled upstairs with Nog to do homework. Mitch had spent the evening playing video games and swearing at the TV. That was Thursday night. Friday night was bound to be a different story. Mitch had packed a substantial amount of alcohol into the fridge as soon as their mom left. "Some friends are coming over while the old lady's gone," he'd explained.

Kailey rotated in her seat to face him. "Okay, why not?"

"My brother's over," he whispered back.

"Where's your mom?"

"Helping my aunt. She just had a baby. She'll be back Saturday sometime."

"Cool. Did your aunt have a boy or a girl?"

Logan shrugged and sat back in his seat.

"How can you not know?"

"I don't care."

"Good morning, class!" Mr. Marksdale entered and Kailey turned around to face the front. Logan studied the back of her head for a moment. Her hair fell in messy ringlets down her back. He glanced at the back of Mazie's head; two pens stuck out of two pink and blue pigtails with a purple polka-dotted bandana tied above her forehead. He wrinkled his nose and moved to look around Kailey's head to see Mr. Marksdale.

That night, Chelsey lay on her back in bed. "What are they doing over there?" she whispered to Kailey.

"I don't know. I've been with you," Kailey whispered back.

Crash!

"What was that?" Chelsey asked.

"It sounded like breaking glass. Oh, and now they're shouting about something again, and laughing. I guess breaking glass is funny."

Chelsey sat up. "Do you think Logan is okay?"

"I think you should go to sleep."

"I think we should pray for everyone over there. Logan's brother is mean."

"How do you know that?" Kailey hissed.

"Logan said so. I met him. He wanted to help build the snowman, but Logan told him to go away." Chelsey bit her lip in the darkness. "I really hope he's okay. Logan used to be mean, too, but I think God is changing him. Like a miracle. Now I won't be able to sleep unless I know he'll be okay."

"Chelsey, I'm sure Logan can take care of himself. If he needs us, he'll come over."

"You think so?"

"Well, he's been here for supper twice now, and I think he likes our family, so I'm pretty sure he would come over if he wasn't safe there. He knows he's safe here."

"But it's the middle of the night." Chelsey sniffed.

"He'll be fine. I love you more than little boys love mud."

"Love you more than girls love dolls."

"Love you more than boys love trucks and tractors."

"Love you more than girls love tea parties."

"Love you more than boys love cookies."

"Love you more than girls love bossing boys." Chelsey yawned and rolled over. "Goodnight, Kailey."

"Goodnight." Kailey lay on her back. It wasn't long till she heard her sister's rhythmic breathing. The crashing and banging continued. "Lord," Kailey prayed, looking at the ceiling, "would you please be with Logan and everyone else in that house tonight? You know what they need. Please just protect them. Thank you. Amen."

"Where's Chelsey?" Kailey asked sleepily the next morning when she walked into the kitchen in her green and red plaid pajama pants and hooded yellow sweater. She'd tossed and turned all night, and still felt tired. Her hair was pulled out of her eyes with a pink headband, but from behind the headband it exploded like a lion's mane after a perm.

"She went over to see Logan. I think she said something about making sure he was alright," Mom answered, sipping her coffee.

"Alone?" Kailey asked in alarm, remembering Logan's request that she not come over.

"No, Dad went with her."

"Good." Kailey poured some Honey Nut Cheerios into a bowl and reached for the milk.

"He means a lot to her, Kailey," Mom said seriously.

"He's her dad. Why wouldn't he?"

"I meant Logan. She prays for him a lot and spends as much time with him as possible."

"I can't figure out why. He's not very nice to her sometimes." Kailey filled her mouth with Cheerios.

"I think it's because he treats her like she's a normal person. He yells at her, laughs at her, laughs with her, and tells her to go away when he's sick of her. That's how she treats him, too."

"I guess." Kailey's toes were getting cold. She finished her food and put her dishes in the sink. "I'll go get dressed, then help you clean up for tomorrow." She stretched with a yawn. "Chelsey's a pretty amazing person, hey Mom?"

"Yes, she is. And you are too."

"Thanks, it's 'cause we have such a good mother." She winked at her mother and went to find her jeans.

CHAPTER THIRTY-SIX

Logan answered the door in his rumpled jeans and wrinkled dress shirt. He hadn't showered and thanks to the remaining gel his hair stuck out in all directions like a porcupine. He opened the door just enough to stick his head out. He groaned when he saw Chelsey's dad standing with her on the step. He knew she would be there—the doorbell gave it away—but her father was not an added bonus in his mind.

"Hi!" Chelsey greeted. "We came to make sure you were okay. We heard a lot of yelling and crashing noises last night. Are you okay?"

"I'm fine," he answered, looking from daughter to father. "Was that all you wanted?"

"No. May we come inside?"

"No. You can ask from right there."

The party the night before had gotten a little out of hand. Mitch's friends had brought their own beer and now the house was a wreck. He had put some of his brother's friends in cabs himself and then settled Mitch in his own bed before falling into bed himself. He had no idea how he was going to get it all straightened out before his mother came home that afternoon, but he knew it would be an all-day task. He hoped she wouldn't be early.

"Okay." Chelsey looked disappointed, but she perked up. "Do you want to come to church tomorrow?"

"No."

She frowned.

"I don't do church."

"Are you scared of church?"

"No."

"Then why won't you come?"

"Sorry, I have to go." He nodded to Mr. Martin and shut the door. He heard the bell ring as he walked away, but he ignored it. Milk and waffles. That was the first thing on his list for the morning. Then he'd try to locate a bucket and some soap.

Kailey slid the cookie batter off the spoon to join the other eleven dots of dough on the baking sheet. The timer on the oven sounded. She pulled on her rooster oven mitt to trade the tray in the oven for the one on the counter.

"Hot, hot," she muttered to herself and left the pan to cool on the top of the stove while she turned her attention to the dishes. The smell of cinnamon and baking filled the quiet kitchen, adding a special kind of warmth. Everyone else was preoccupied with a movie Uncle Bruno had dropped off earlier.

The timer sounded again, and she had just taken the last batch out when the phone rang. Kailey pulled off her oven mitt and picked up the phone.

"Hello?"

"Hey, Kailey? Um...are you busy?"

"Logan?" *Why is Logan calling and asking if I'm busy?*

"Yeah, it's me." She heard him sigh. "Are you busy?"

"You mean like, *right* now?"

"Yeah."

"Why?" she asked tentatively, leaning on the countertop.

"Well, my brother, Mitch, had a party last night..."

"Yeah, we heard."

"Oh, well, he's getting over a hangover right now and they made a big mess and my mom's coming home this afternoon. I need help."

Kailey was quiet for a moment. *Love your enemies. Love your enemies. But I don't want to go over there and help. Let him clean up his own mess. It's not my problem. But then his mom will come home to a disaster.*

"Kailey?"

"I'm still here." She had to make a decision. "Go find another pair of gloves. I'll be right over."

She heard him exhale slowly. "Thank you."

She laughed. "Don't thank me yet. Be over in a minute." She hung up and whispered to her mother about where she was going. Then she found her coat and hat, grabbed two fresh cookies, and left her safe, warm house.

"Wow." Kailey stood in the Stewart's front room staring at the mess before her. She handed Logan a cookie and took a step further into the room. Several pieces of furniture lay on their sides, and most were missing a leg or two. Yellow spots splattered the wall behind the couch, and shreds of cloth from the torn drapes littered the floor along with beer cans and bottles.

"Did they just stand against this wall and spit alcohol at it?" she asked, climbing over a broken armchair to get a better look.

"They must have been telling jokes," he answered sheepishly.

"I don't think we'll be able to get rid of that without painting over it. How are you going to fix the furniture?"

He shrugged.

She wrinkled her nose. "It stinks in here, like beer and barf and smoke. Were they smoking in your mom's living room?"

"Probably."

"Well, how about we pick up the garbage first and then wash the walls and floors? Do you have any encyclopedias?"

"What?"

"We can put them under the furniture till someone has time to fix the actual legs," Kailey said. "Assuming you guys don't use your encyclopedias every day." She smirked.

Logan shared a small smile. "No, not every day."

"Okay, well, let's start with the garbage?"

Logan handed her a black bag and then went to the garage to get boxes for the bottles and cans. They stacked the full boxes in the garage so that they could take them down to the beer store after everything was cleaned up.

"We might as well make some money on this," Logan said.

Next, they both pulled on rubber gloves and wiped down the walls in the living room. Logan turned on the radio to a rock station and Kailey asked him to change it so they could hear Uncle Bruno. Once the windows, walls, floors, and other surfaces were clean in the living room, kitchen, and entranceway, they turned their attention to the worst room of all: the bathroom.

"Why do people get drunk in the first place?" Kailey pushed the plunger into the toilet. "What's the point of drinking so much that you can't remember what you did and you have a headache and you throw up? None of those things sound fun to me."

Logan was scrubbing some vomit off the wall. He'd been drunk once or twice, but he wasn't going to confess that to Kailey. He was angry. Angry at Mitch for being so stupid, angry at his mom for leaving him with this mess, and angry at Kailey for helping clean up a disgusting situation that she had nothing to do with. He wasn't sure why that angered him, but it did.

"Did your dad go with your mom, and that's why he wasn't here?"

Kailey's question was the last straw that set off the bomb of his anger. "No," he retorted, working on the wall's stain with extra force. "He hasn't gone anywhere with my mom for like two years." He turned to her. "Yeah, that's right, Kailey. Not everyone has a perfect little family like yours. Some of us live in a real world where their parents care more about money and the hot secretary they hired than their own kids. So you can go on in your perfect life with your perfect friends and family and *church*, but that's not reality. None of those things really exist. Friends are a joke. They're just people who can benefit from you in some way. Family's just a bunch of blood relations that use you because they can, and they can always come back to use you because they're related. And church, *church* is full of judgmental perfectionists who look down their noses at everyone else.

"Don't you dare judge me, Kailey Martin, for the way I live because I'm willing to bet my life is a whole lot harder than yours." Logan's eyes flashed in anger. "I hate my dad. I hate him more than I have ever hated anyone else in my entire life, and that's saying a lot because I've hated a lot of people." He swore and punched the wall.

Kailey slid onto the floor beside Logan. He was breathing heavily.

"Even when he lived here, nothing was ever good enough for him. Mom didn't make enough money, Mom didn't cook good enough food, I wasn't smart enough, I wasn't good at sports, I didn't have enough friends or go to enough cool parties—nothing was ever enough for him. He worked all the time. All the time. He would leave for work early and have meetings almost every night of the week and on weekends. And then Mom found out he was cheating on her with the secretary at work." Logan took a deep breath. "She confronted him about it. I was in my bedroom upstairs and heard her yell through the vents. Then—"

He stopped.

Kailey waited.

Her bottom was getting cold from sitting on the tile floor. The air was filled with vomit and ammonium, stinging the inside of her nose. Still, she waited.

"Then I heard him hit her. He hit her hard. I was so scared. I crouched down between my bed and the wall, right over the vent. I heard her say something and then he hit her again and she screamed. A couple minutes later, the door slammed shut. It shook the entire house. I got up and lay in bed and tried to sleep. The next morning Mom looked really sad, like she had cried all night. And Dad never came back."

Kailey felt tears come to her eyes. She looked at Logan to see him studying his feet. His eyes were dry and his face was hard. She looked away and then said what was on her heart.

"My dad died."

She said it quietly, but Logan caught her words and his head snapped up. "What?"

Kailey sniffed. "It's true. My dad, my biological dad, died when I was six. He had cancer." Her voice broke on the word. "He was really sick. I remember visiting him in this white room. He was covered in tubes and he was missing all his hair. He was really weak. A picture Chelsey and I drew for him was beside his bed.

"He loved us a lot." Tears slid down her cheeks. "He always told us, 'I love you more than caterpillars and hotdogs,' things like that. He was so brave, Logan, and when he died and went to live with Jesus I thought my heart would never mend. My hero was gone and he was never, *ever* coming home."

Logan sat on the floor and stared at her. Tears poured down her face.

"Bill, my new dad, went to our church. He and Mom got married a year later, and Devin was born a year after that." She wiped her cheek and met his eyes. "You're right, I don't know what it's like to be you. My dad didn't walk out on us. He loved us until the day he died, literally, and our new dad loves us a lot, too. And I am so very sorry that all those things had to happen to you. I'm sorry your father hurt you so much. Truly I am. But Logan, just because your dad doesn't love you doesn't mean you aren't loved."

Logan looked away.

"Chelsey loves you. My family loves you. God loves you. Chelsey loved you when you were mean to her. God loves you even though you don't obey Him. And…" Kailey swallowed. "I am sorry that I've judged you and not shown you the same kind of love that God has shown to me. Will you forgive me?"

Logan stared at Kailey's face, now red from crying. He nodded.

She smiled and pulled him into a hug.

He sat for a moment in shock, and then let his tears flow. He didn't remember the last time he had received such a gentle embrace. The two teens sat on the bathroom floor in the midst of buckets and soap and dirt, and Kailey's arms stayed around Logan as they cried. He wasn't sure how long they sat there, but Kailey pulled herself together first and let go of him. She reached for a piece of toilet paper to wipe her eyes and handed him some as well.

"Thanks," he muttered.

She blew her nose and mopped her tears. "Wow," she breathed, and looked at him and then back at her hands. "Thanks."

He stood and offered her his hand. She took it and he pulled her up. They completed cleaning the bathroom without further conversation. When it smelled like soap again, they retreated to the entranceway.

Logan surveyed their work. The house looked much closer to its normal self now that encyclopedias held up the furniture and the beer bottles were gone. It smelled heavily like lemon and pine, but that was an improvement from the morning. Bruno's voice came over the radio, announcing an approaching snowstorm for that evening.

"I think my work here is done," Kailey said.

"Thank you, Kailey."

"You're welcome." Her green eyes held a peaceful look. She sat on the bench near the door and pulled on her boots. "Oh, and I don't know what you're doing for the holidays, but I think Mom was going to ask if you and your mom wanted to come over on Tuesday night for supper. Uncle Bruno and Aunt Louise are coming, too."

"I'll ask Mom when she gets back."

"Okay, see you, and good luck when she comes home." Kailey stood still for a moment, then she walked up to Logan and gave him a warm hug. She stepped back with a smile and then stepped out the door with a little wave before returning to her house.

CHAPTER THIRTY-SEVEN

Logan and Mrs. Stewart arrived for dinner shortly before 5:30 on Tuesday. Louise let them in, and led Mrs. Stewart down the hallway to the right of the staircase to the kitchen in order to avoid the wrestling in the living room. Logan was not so fortunate, as Devin had heard the doorbell and hardly gave him time to remove his boots and coat before pulling him to the floor. Bruno and Chelsey were quick to follow. Mrs. Martin called a halt to their match, however, when they nearly knocked over the Christmas tree.

What a Christmas tree it was. You could hardy tell what the tree itself looked like thanks to the lights and ornaments, most of them homemade. Chelsey explained that they emptied the ornament box every year and put each one on the tree. What was the point of having so many decorations if you didn't use them all?

Kailey called them to sit down for dinner. She took Chelsey's outreached hand and gave Logan a friendly push. He smiled and followed the pair into the kitchen. Dinner was quite a feast: plates and bowls were piled high with fluffy mashed potatoes, gravy, apple sauce, green beans with toasted almonds, honeyed carrots, and a vibrant salad. In the centre of it all, the largest roast turkey Logan had ever seen. Mrs. Stewart asked for the stuffing recipe at one point, and Mrs. Martin handed her the box. Logan was working on his second helping of stuffing and nodded his approval.

After dinner, they retired to the living room for chocolate cake and ice cream. Once everyone was seated with their dessert and coffee or tea, Chelsey started to giggle.

"What?" Logan asked, staring at her.

She shook her head, her eyes locked on Dad.

"Why's she giggling?" Logan asked.

"Because she thinks something's funny," Kailey replied in a serious tone, but her eyes gave away that she also knew of a private joke.

"What?"

"Well, isn't that why you tend to giggle?" Uncle Bruno asked, slapping his back.

Logan cocked his head to one side. He looked at his mother and exchanged a shrug with her.

"You better just tell them, dear, before they think we've gone completely mad and run away home." Mrs. Martin touched her husband's arm gently. All eyes turned to Bill Martin.

He cleared his throat. "Every year at Christmas, the Martin and Cowden families give gifts, not only to each other but to whoever happens to be in our home. Every year we do it a bit differently, mostly just depending on how we feel at any given moment. At this moment, we'd like to give away a few, particularly a few things we stole from people. Bruno, you may go first."

Uncle Bruno's auburn eyes were shining with laughter. He pulled a stuffed hippo from behind his back. Logan stared on in confusion and Kailey gasped. Uncle Bruno grinned and threw it to her. "This gift is for Kailey. I didn't want to take anything from my lovely, patient, long-suffering wife, so I snuck into your room and stole it off your bed."

"Thanks for returning it." Kailey stuck out her tongue.

"I don't understand," Mrs. Stewart said.

"Every year we take things from people and then give them back before Christmas," Devin said.

"Why?" asked Logan.

"I had a hard time with this, too, when I came into this family," Aunt Louise volunteered.

"It's a tradition that Jack and I started," Bruno said. "When we were kids—"

"And in college," Mrs. Martin interjected.

"And in college. Okay, pretty much our entire lives. We were too cheap to buy gifts for each other, so we'd just steal things from the other person and wrap them and then return them at Christmas. Now it's just fun. We give real gifts, too. Sometimes we do a prize for the person who stole the best thing or had it for the longest. You just can't steal money, I think that's the only rule."

Suddenly a light went on in Logan's head. Devin had gotten up to return something to their mother, so he leaned over and whispered to Kailey, "Was Jack your first father and Bruno's brother?"

She nodded. "They were twins."

Logan sat back and nodded.

"I think I win for the best thing and the longest thing," Chelsey said. "Logan."

He looked up.

"Your bike is in our garage." Everyone stared at her. "It's been there since I think October 4."

"Chelsey!" Mrs. Martin scolded.

"It's not money. That's fair. And I have another gift for all of you. Be right back." She walked away to her room.

The five adults all held expressions of wonder. "Did she really have your bike for that long?" Aunt Louise asked.

Logan nodded. "Why else would I have had to walk with them?"

Bruno started to laugh. "What a smart girl! She gets that from me."

This comment started an argument that still wasn't resolved when Chelsey returned holding a thin rectangle wrapped in brown paper.

"Everyone, this is for our family. Our project for art class was to paint what was important to each of us. This is what I painted. Devin, would you rip the paper?"

He happily complied.

Everyone grew quiet and stared. The picture was of the front of the Martin's house in the autumn. Mr. and Mrs. Martin stood beside the maple tree in the front lawn, looking away from the house. Devin, Chelsey, and Uncle Bruno were playing in a pile of leaves. Aunt Louise stood beside a stroller on the driveway, and Logan and Kailey stood beside her, talking.

"Logan, you're part of our family now," Chelsey announced. "And Mrs. Stewart, I will paint you in somewhere, too. You both belong with us. Merry Christmas."

"Merry Christmas," everyone echoed, and more cake was served all around.

"Kailey?"

"What, Chelsey?" Kailey whispered back in the darkness of their bedroom that night after the visitors had gone home and the house was quiet.

"Do you think Mrs. Stewart and Logan liked my painting?"

"Yes."

"I'm glad. Did you like it?"

"Yes."

"Do you think Logan loves Jesus?"

"No, but that doesn't mean he never will. Logan has a sad story. You were right, Chelsey, we need to love him and pray for him. I'm sorry I didn't listen to you."

"I forgive you. You love him and pray for him now, right?"

"I try to."

"That's good. It's almost New Year's."

Kailey waited.

"We get to start driving next year."

Kailey moaned and rolled over. "I don't think Dad will let you drive anything."

"Probably not. But I can still scream when you drive."

"Thanks," Kailey muttered sarcastically. "Love you more than a fat kid loves cake."

"I love you more than Santa probably loves cake."

"I think he eats lots of candy canes, actually—and eggnog."

"Yuck!" Chelsey made a gagging sound.

"Goodnight, girls!" Dad yelled through the door.

"Goodnight!" They both yelled back.

Kailey lay in the darkness. Driving started in May. What an adventure that would be.

Chelsey must have still been thinking about Santa, because just before Kailey fell asleep, she heard Chelsey roll over and mutter, "Egg-nog. Yuck."

Watch for other books in the
ANOTHER DAY IN BENTON series